JESSICA BECK

THE DONUT MYSTERIES, BOOK 39

CARAMEL CANVAS

The First Time Ever Published!

The 39th Donut Mystery.

Jessica Beck is the *New York Times* Bestselling Author of the
Donut Mysteries, the Classic Diner Mysteries, the Ghost
Cat Cozy Mysteries, and the Cast Iron Cooking Mysteries.

For P & E,
For being there for me through it all, from the very beginning!

When Suzanne Hart returns to April Springs after being away, she learns that one of her good friends, artist Annabeth Kline, has died by accident in her studio, but as Suzanne looks deeper into the situation, it quickly becomes clear to her that Annabeth's death was no accident!

CHAPTER 1

WHEN MY HUSBAND AND I finally returned to April Springs after two solid months of a long and slow healing process for me—both for my once-broken arm *and* my shattered peace of mind—Jake and I soon found out that a lot had been going on in April Springs during the time we'd been away. That's the way it is sometimes. The world keeps spinning, and people continue living their own lives, whether we are there to be a part of them or not.

I just didn't expect to discover that one of my dear friends had died while we'd been away.

What made it somehow even worse was that it happened a week *before* Jake and I made it back into town.

If only we'd cut our trip a few days short.

If I'd just had the foresight to call a few people while I'd been away to tell them how much I loved them, losing her might not have felt so rotten to me.

If. If. If.

Wishing for what could never be was no way to live my life, ruefully hoping that I'd done things differently, and besides, I'd been in a dark place for a long time, nearly losing my own life. I'd been torn apart, and I'd needed time alone—well, with Jake anyway—to try to put myself back together again.

I thought I'd finally managed to do it, and then I found my mother sitting on the front porch of the cottage we'd once shared. I hadn't been expecting a welcome-home party. In fact,

1

I'd insisted that everyone pretend I'd never even been away, but finding her grim countenance staring at me as we got out of Jake's truck brought me crashing back to reality quicker than I'd wanted.

"Suzanne, welcome back," Momma said as she hugged me gently, being careful of my now-healed arm.

"It's okay to squeeze me tighter than that," I said. "My arm is fine now," I said as I demonstrated a full range of motion. The rehabilitation exercises had been tortuous at times, but I'd been determined to make myself as good as new again. After all, though most folks didn't realize it, making donuts was a physically demanding job, and the only thing in the world I desperately wanted to do at that moment was to get back to work at Donut Hearts.

"I can't help myself," she said, clinging to me a bit longer and harder than needed, even though I hadn't seen her in so long.

"I'll just grab our bags while you two say hello," Jake said, clearly trying to give us some time alone together.

"Stay right where you are, young man," Momma said as she broke free of me and gave my husband a quicker, though just as heartfelt, embrace than she'd given me.

"Momma, what's wrong?" I asked, looking deep into her eyes.

"We don't need to talk about it out here," my mother said as she took my hand in hers. "Let's go inside first. I know you didn't want me to do anything special, but I made you a pie. You don't have to eat it if you don't want to."

"I can personally assure you that there's no chance of that happening, Dot," Jake said with a wry smile. If there was anyone in the world who loved my mother's baking more than I did, it had to be my husband.

I looked around at the empty park that surrounded our

cottage. "Momma, why are you being so mysterious? There's no one within half a mile of us right now. Talk to me."

"Suzanne, I'm afraid I've got some terrible news. I wish I could spare you the pain on your homecoming, but you're going to find out soon enough, and I wanted to be the one to break it to you."

I felt a sudden dread sweep through me. "Momma, it's not like you to beat around the bush. Tell me what happened." A sudden thought swept into my mind unbidden. "Did something happen to Grace or George or Trish?" I looked around. "Where's Phillip?" Had her husband had a heart attack in our absence?

"They're all fine," Momma said, squeezing my hand a little tighter than she had before. My dear sweet mother, for one moment looking every minute of her age, took a deep breath, and then she steeled herself as she said, "Suzanne, I'm so sorry to have to be the one to tell you this.

"Annabeth Kline is dead."

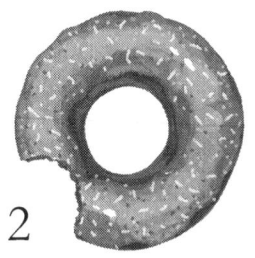

CHAPTER 2

HAT DO YOU MEAN, ANNABETH is dead?" I asked, feeling the strength leave my legs. "What happened to her? When?" Annabeth had been a friend of mine since our school days. Once upon a time we'd both dreamed of being famous artists, and while my career path had ultimately led me into donut making, Annabeth had stayed true to her original calling. She'd had her own share of struggles along the way, even painting the donut shop window for her very first commission out of college, but she'd finally succeeded, and her art and her custom logos were all over the world now, for all of the good it ended up doing her. "She brought me a painting for the shop not two weeks ago. I didn't even know it was ready. In fact, I wasn't entirely sure at the time that she wasn't joking about doing it. Annabeth offered to paint it for free donuts, just like the old days. Emma brought it over here to the cottage as soon as Annabeth delivered it, but I haven't even seen it yet," I explained. I'd asked for my privacy when I'd left April Springs in ruins, but Emma had ignored my request when the painting had arrived at Donut Hearts. She thought I'd want to know, but Jake had a firm but gentle conversation with her, and that phone call telling me about the painting's delivery had been her last one to me. "How did it happen, Momma?"

"Evidently she was climbing up into her loft in her studio when the ladder gave way. I heard that it was old and practically worn out, but she'd kept it for its charm. What made things

worse was that her poor dear mother was the one who found her. Alyssa is still in shock. I tried to reach out to her a couple of times, but she politely declined. When I told her that I was going to call you to come to the funeral, she told me not to do it. She said that Annabeth had cherished your friendship, and that her daughter had recently told her that she wanted at least one of her close friends to not be a part of saying good-bye to her. It didn't make any sense to me, but I decided to respect the sentiment. I hope you can find it in your heart to forgive me." Momma looked as though she was the one that was about to cry.

I put my arms around her. "It's okay. You did the right thing."

"But you didn't get to say good-bye," Momma said through her tears.

"I'm just happy I could do one last thing for her," I said.

Jake coughed politely as we all walked up onto the porch, and then he pulled out his cell phone.

"Who are you calling?"

"I'm cancelling the job, Suzanne."

"What job?" Momma asked.

"It's not important now," Jake replied.

"It surely is," I said, putting my hand on his to stop him from making that call. "Jake, you need to do this."

"Suzanne, Tommy can find someone else. I need to be with you right now." His tone of voice was emphatic, but I wasn't going to let that stop me.

"Momma, would you warm up three slices of pie for us? We'll be inside in a minute."

My mother took the hint immediately. "Of course."

Once she was in the cottage, I turned to my husband and said, "Don't cancel, Jake."

"Suzanne, you just lost your friend."

"She's been gone for a week," I said stoically. "I wouldn't want to face her funeral without you, but that's a moot point

now. You've been taking care of me nonstop for two months. You need to do this for you."

"It wasn't as though it was a burden or anything," he said softly.

"Maybe not, but I know there were times when you were ready to run away screaming," I corrected him, not allowing him to gloss over my periods of melancholy and my intermittent sullen refusal to do my exercises.

"Well, maybe not screaming," he replied with the first hint of a smile I'd seen in a while.

"But running, nonetheless," I answered, kissing him lightly to show him that I was just teasing. "Jake, there's another reason you should do this. I don't have to remind you that we haven't had any money coming in for two months while we've been away. Emma and Sharon have been splitting the profits from the shop, which is only fair, and you've been taking care of me. Honestly, the best thing I can do at the moment is get back to work, and the same thing goes for you."

"I don't want to leave you," he said softly. "I've really enjoyed the past two months."

"So have I, but don't worry. We'll have plenty of time together soon enough," I replied as I patted his shoulder. "The original plan was that you were going to leave as soon as I got settled, so I don't see any reason to change that now."

"I feel like a bad husband deserting you in your time of need." He said it with such sadness in his voice that I knew I had to be gentle with him.

"Jake, my dear sweet husband, you just spent the last two months helping me put myself back together. I'm finally whole again. You have been the best husband any woman could ask for. Now it's time for you to go."

He laughed at the seeming juxtaposition of my statements. "You sure don't mind sending mixed messages, do you?" Taking

my hands in his, he asked, "Are you certain this is what you want?"

"I'm positive," I said.

Jake still seemed to hesitate, and then he asked, "I can still have my pie first though, right?"

"You can take it *all* with you," I said. "Well, all that's left, anyway."

My husband hugged me fiercely, and I was glad that *he* wasn't afraid of hurting me. He, more than anyone, knew just how far I'd come. "I love you, young lady."

"I love you too, kind sir," I answered.

When we walked inside the cottage, Momma was waiting for us, though she was carefully pretending not to even be aware of our presence. "The pie is ready."

"Jake is leaving," I said, blurting it out as was my custom.

"Jake?" Momma asked him.

"Dot, I agreed to take on a job in Tennessee before we knew about Annabeth. I wanted to stay, but Suzanne made some good points about why it might be good for me to go. What do you think?"

Before my mother could answer, I stepped between the two of them. "Jake Bishop, you did *not* just ask my mother for her approval. I'm sure I didn't hear that correctly."

Momma said seriously, "I don't know what you're talking about. I didn't hear anything. Do you have time for pie before you go, Jake?"

"That would be great," my husband said, clearly grateful for escape from the trap he'd set for himself. As I went to get us milk for the pie, I saw Momma whisper something to Jake that made him smile.

"What are you two conspiring about?" I asked them with mock severity in my tone.

"Nothing," Jake said.

"Nothing that concerns *you*," Momma amended, and then she laughed, a sound I'd missed since I'd been away. "I was going to skip having any pie myself, but it smelled so good that I decided to join you, if that's all right."

"All right? It's perfect," I said as I hugged her yet again.

As we ate the delightful baked treat, Momma said, "Suzanne, if you don't want to rattle around in this cottage all by yourself while Jake is gone, you're more than welcome to come stay with Phillip and me."

"Thanks. I appreciate the offer, but I'm staying right where I am. I've been dying to get back to feeling truly at home again. This cottage has everything I need."

"Our place isn't exactly a cave, you know," Momma said a little defensively, and then she backpedaled. "I understand, though. This is where you grew up. Why *wouldn't* you rather stay here? I can still visit you though, right?"

"Any time," I said, and when I saw her eyes light up, I quickly added, "within reason."

We all laughed at that, and too soon, our pie was gone and Jake was on his way out the door.

"I'll walk you out," I said.

"Jake, it was lovely seeing you again, however briefly," Momma said.

"Thanks again for the pie," he said. "If it weren't so good, I'd feel guilty about taking the rest of it with me, but I know you can always make more, whereas my supply is severely limited."

"Taking what is left is the highest compliment you can pay me," she said.

At the truck, Jake threw his bag onto the passenger seat I had so recently occupied myself. At least the cabin we'd been

staying in had a laundry room, so I was sending him off with clean clothes. "Call me the second you get there, and be careful in that truck of yours, especially if it snows."

"That's what the weight in back is for, and the snow chains, too," he said. "I'll be fine. Are you sure you will be?"

"Absolutely," I answered.

After one last long and lingering kiss, he was on his way. I watched until his taillights disappeared around the corner, and then I rejoined Momma inside. I loved my husband dearly, and the time we'd spent together had been priceless, but I'd meant what I'd said.

We both needed to get on with our lives, and the sooner we made that happen, the better.

"How are you feeling, Suzanne?" Momma asked me not a minute after Jake left.

"I'm fine," I said, not even pausing to think about it. I *was* fine, not normal, not perfect, not spectacular, but fine. It was all that I could muster at the time after all that I'd been through.

"Talk to me, dear sweet daughter," Momma urged.

"It's hard," I finally admitted. "I'm not sure I could have put myself back together without Jake." I was suddenly aware of how that must sound to her. "I don't mean that *you* couldn't have done it," I quickly amended.

Momma smiled softly. "Suzanne, if your husband isn't the main source of stability in your life, you probably chose the wrong man. I heartily approve of him, you know, as if it matters at this point."

"What did you whisper to him?" I asked her, suddenly needing to hear her answer.

"I promised him that we would take care of you while he was gone," Momma said, and then, before I could respond, she

quickly added, "Not that you need all that much taking care of. I know you're a grown woman, but I still can't help thinking of you at times as my little girl. Sometimes I find myself wishing that I could take you in my lap, kiss your booboo, hold you tight, and tell you how much I love you."

"You can still do all of that," I said with a smile. "Though I might crush you a bit at this weight."

It was her turn to laugh. "I'm willing to risk the potential injuries if you need it," she answered, "though if you ask me, you're practically wasting away."

I had lost several pounds while I'd been gone, but I wasn't sure they'd stay off once I got back to the donut shop full time. "Just having you here is all that I need." I paused for a few moments as I stared into the fire. We were in the coldest season of our year—Christmas and New Year's had come and gone while Jake and I had been away—but somehow it was okay. There had still been plenty to celebrate, but I hadn't wanted to even acknowledge it while we'd been away.

"Are you okay with Jake leaving you here alone? Honestly?" she asked me.

"The truth is that I'm happy he's got something important to do," I said. "What do *you* really think?"

"Not that it's any business of mine, but it seems to me like it is something you both need," Momma answered.

"That's not really an answer though, is it?" I probed a little deeper.

"Maybe not, but it's the best one you're going to get out of me." Momma sipped her tea and then added, "I should have baked *two* pies."

"Why, are you honestly still hungry?" I asked her, amazed that this little woman could eat more after the massive slices we'd had earlier.

"No, of course not, but what will you do if you want another slice later?"

I reached over and patted her hand. "Momma, I'll be just f... dandy," I said, cancelling the word *fine* as it started to leave my lips. "I can go to the store tomorrow and stock up on everything I need."

She looked clearly guilty about something, and I suspected I knew what it was. Without a word, I got up and walked into the kitchen. My freezer was packed with meals that hadn't been there before, including homemade bread.

Momma spoke from just behind me as she said, "I may have gotten a little carried away, but I didn't want you to come back to a bare freezer."

"I appreciate that," I said, feeling relief that my mother could be a little overbearing at times. There were occasions, like at that particular moment, that it was exactly what I needed, though I would never have admitted it under interrogation.

"You might not want to look in the fridge," Momma suggested as she bit her lower lip.

Of course I immediately opened the fridge's door. It, too, was full of food, ready to pop into an oven to warm up at a moment's notice. With Jake gone, I wouldn't have to cook for myself for a month. I didn't honestly mind that much, though. Momma was one of my favorite cooks in the world.

I turned and hugged her. "Thanks for looking out for me."

"It's what I do," my mother said. As I held her, I realized yet again what a small woman she was in physical stature. Her personality was so large that sometimes it made it difficult to remember just how tiny she was. I had inherited none of that. I had that chunky physique that my father and his brothers had. Lucky me. "Suzanne, I wasn't kidding before. You are absolutely wasting away. Didn't you two eat *anything* while you were gone?"

I had to laugh. "We ate plenty, but Jake's idea of mending

my body and soul was to take long hikes in the woods every single day, whether it was sunny or raining, cloudy or clear. He even dragged me out a few times in the snow."

"You love snow," Momma said with a smile.

"True, but I enjoy it more when I'm inside by a fire looking out a window than traipsing across the countryside in it."

"Well, you're home now," Momma said. "That's what counts."

"In more ways than one," I said as we walked back into the living room together. I'd loved the cabin where we'd stayed, on Momma's dime no less, but there was no place like home. "By the way, thanks again for financing our trip."

"Suzanne, you're most welcome, but you need to stop thanking me. It was the least I could do."

"I don't know about that," I said. "We never could have afforded it on our own." Momma looked as though she was suddenly uncomfortable by the turn our conversation had taken. "What is it?"

"How are you set, financially? You know, I'd be more than happy to help out, just until you get back on your feet again." Before I could protest, she added, "I know how you feel about accepting gifts, so we could call it a loan if you'd like. You might as well get a little of your inheritance early, as far as I'm concerned," she added softly.

"Thanks, but that's a hard no." I hated when my mother acknowledged her own mortality. I refused to believe there would ever be a time in my life when she wasn't around, no matter how foolish that basic premise might have been.

There was still a little a bit of tension between us when I heard someone knocking on the front door. I couldn't face anyone at the moment, and I had hoped my well-meaning friends understood that. "Momma, would you get that? I can't deal with anyone right now."

"Certainly," Momma said, putting on her fiercest expression

as she walked to the front door. Despite her petite size, no one ever mistook my mother for a pushover, and from the look of determination on her face, I could see that wasn't about to change now.

To my surprise, Momma didn't immediately rebuff whoever was standing outside. "Suzanne, are you *sure* you don't want to see anybody?"

I thought about it, and then I realized that there was one other person I could be myself with, warts and all. "Unless it's Grace, send them away please."

She must have heard her name from the porch. "You're in luck then, aren't you?" Grace came in, grinned at me, and then hugged me harder than she ever had in her life. She was clearly not worried about hurting me, though I wondered how my ribs would stand up under the onslaught. "I missed you," she said fiercely. "Don't ever do that again."

"I'll try not to," I said. "Would you mind easing up a bit?"

"Did I hurt your arm?" she asked as she pulled back suddenly.

"No, but I might have a few cracked ribs after that bear hug of yours."

Grace laughed, and I realized how much I'd missed my best friend while I'd been away. She was more than a sister could have been to me; we were close by choice, not some freak genetic lottery, and I loved her all the more for it. She suddenly got serious. "You heard about Annabeth, didn't you?"

"I told her myself," Momma said.

"We wanted to call you, but Alyssa was pretty insistent about it. I didn't get it. You and Annabeth were close. Sure, we were friends, but you two bonded over your art from way back. I felt so guilty when I heard that she had died."

"Why is that?" I asked, clearly confused by Grace's statement.

"I always resented her a little for the time she took you away from me," my best friend admitted. "It's pretty shallow and

13

petty of me now, but I couldn't help myself back then. I just wish I'd apologized to her when I'd had the chance. Now I can never make amends."

"Grace, she didn't hold anything against you. We talked about you six months ago, and she had nothing but respect and admiration in her voice when she spoke of you. She was so impressed with how well you'd done with your life."

"Me? I work a job. She created art. Annabeth was the impressive one. I still can't believe she's gone."

"I can't either," I said as I walked over and touched the plain brown-paper-wrapped painting leaning in the hallway. "She painted this for me, you know."

"Don't you want to open it?" Grace asked eagerly.

"Not just yet," I said. "I'm not sure I can handle it. By the way, how did you know that we were back?"

"I saw you drive up, and I was about to crash your homecoming when I saw Jake drive back down the road in his truck not fifteen minutes later. I flagged him down, and he told me everything. That was all the motivation I needed to hightail it up here and see how you were doing for myself." She took a few steps back and pretended to appraise me. "You could put on a few pounds," she finally said judiciously.

"I don't know. I kind of like myself this size," I said. Though most of my clothing was loose on me, this was baggy season, where no one really wore formfitting clothes, if you didn't count the leggings that a great many women found fashionable. I for one had never been comfortable wearing them outside of the cottage, but clearly I was in the minority having that opinion.

"If you're going to maintain this weight, we need to go clothes shopping soon," Momma said.

"In that case, I'll start eating immediately. I *hate* shopping," I said, and it was true. I suppose there were a great many ways I was an anomaly, but that suited me just fine. I never minded

being different. In fact, there were many times that I reveled in it.

"You don't have to decide anything today," Momma said as she glanced quickly at her watch.

"Is there somewhere you need to be?" I asked her. "It's okay if there is. You've done more than enough here."

"Suzanne, Phillip can wait for me until I'm ready to go."

"I'll stay, Dot," Grace volunteered. "I took some vacation time I saved up while Suzanne was away. I can't believe how much paid time off they give me. Sometimes it can be a real burden."

I thought about all of the money I'd missed out running Donut Hearts while I'd been away. "Sorry, but I refuse to sympathize with you," I said with a grin.

"It's a worry I bear constantly," Grace said melodramatically. "Seriously, Dot, we'll be fine."

"Very well." She took my hands in hers. "Suzanne, at least come by my place this evening for a proper meal."

"If everything you left me in the fridge and the freezer isn't proper, I'm not sure I know what it is," I said.

"That's for later. I insist," she said before turning to Grace. "You must come, too."

"Well, if I must, I must," Grace replied with a huge grin. "Any chance there will be dessert?"

"You can count on it," Momma said.

It all sounded great, but then the thought of leaving the cottage was suddenly more than I could stand. "Momma, I'm not sure I can go out just yet and face the world."

Thank goodness she didn't make me explain. "That's fine. I'll bring the food to you and we can eat here. Phillip has a new project he's working on, so I'm not even sure he will notice that I'm gone."

"What is it, another cold case?" I asked. My stepfather, once

our chief of police, had found a suitable hobby in retirement, digging into very cold cases and trying to solve them.

"We can talk about all of that later," Momma said. "I'll see you girls at six," she told us, and then she was gone.

CHAPTER 3

"Now, tell me what you've been up to since I've been gone," I said as Grace and I took our usual places in the living room. The fireplace was prominent, which I dearly loved. The crackling logs generated sounds, sights, *and* warmth, something I never grew tired of. The cabin Jake and I had shared had been lovely, even coming with a fireplace of its own, though it was gas, not wood fired. "How's Stephen?"

Grace smiled. "I am happy to report that things have never been better," she said, and I could tell that she clearly meant it.

"I'm so happy for you," I said. "What happened to make him change?"

"Honestly, I think it was what happened to you. After what you went through at the donut shop, he knew that I could have been involved in that mess right beside you, and he decided that he'd better get it together or take a chance on losing me forever."

"I'm glad I could help," I said softly, recalling with a shudder that final confrontation with my attacker, someone I never would have suspected had it in her, and how close she'd come to ending me once and for all.

"You know what I mean. Every cloud has its silver lining and all of that. How are you sleeping these days?"

"Have you been talking to Jake behind my back?" I asked her suddenly.

Grace looked surprised by my reaction. "I swear, the first time I spoke with him since you left was less than an hour ago."

"I'm sorry," I said, reaching out my hand and squeezing hers lightly. "At first I barely slept, but lately I haven't had any flashbacks at all."

"That's good news," she said. "Are you really going back to the donut shop in the morning? Isn't it a little soon?"

"Grace, I've been away for two months. It's time. If I'm ever going to do it, it has to be now."

"I get that," she said. After a few moments of silence, she offered, "Would you like me to get up early and go with you?"

I knew what a sacrifice it was for her to give up so much sleep, a gesture I appreciated more than I could say. "Thanks for the offer, but I have to do this alone."

"I understand," she said. Did she look a little relieved as she said that? Even if it were true, I couldn't hold it against her.

"So, we still have four hours before your mother comes over with dinner. What would you like to do? We can take a drive around town, or just hang around here. It's your call."

"If you don't mind, I don't want to leave the cottage until I have to tomorrow morning. Is that okay with you?"

"Okay? It's perfect." Grace reached into her oversized bag and pulled out half a dozen of our favorite old movies. "Feel like some popcorn and a flick or two?" she asked me.

"That sounds absolutely lovely," I replied. I knew I would have to face the townsfolk of April Springs soon enough, but for now, I just wanted to hang out with my best friend and watch a favorite old movie as though nothing had happened to drive me away for so long. Leave it to Grace to come up with the perfect afternoon.

After watching two romantic comedies in a row, I found myself settling in to the point that, for just a moment, I forgot

everything that had happened in the past two months. Sure, I missed my husband, and oddly enough, the intense time we'd just spent together made me miss him more, not less. It was going to take some getting used to being on my own again, but I knew I'd manage it.

"Are you ladies ready for dinner?" Momma asked with perfect timing not ten minutes after the second movie was over.

"How did you know?" I asked with a grin.

"If memory serves, you two are *always* ready for your next meal," Momma replied. In a gentler voice, she said, "I hope you don't mind, but Phillip begged me to let him come along. He said he wanted to help, but I know it was just an excuse to see you. If you don't want him to come in, just say so and I'll let him know."

It touched me that my former adversary and I had grown so close. When he'd first started to pursue my mother, I was adamantly against it, but over time, I'd learned to see the man in a completely different light. Some of that, maybe not a small part, may have had something to do with the fact that my mother was crazy about him, but there was more to it than that. We'd worked on a few cases together since he'd retired, and we'd each grown to respect the other's abilities. "Let him in. The truth is that I'd love to see him," I said.

Momma touched my cheek lightly as she smiled. "You have a good heart, young lady."

"Hey, the rest of me is not so bad, either," I said jokingly, trying to defuse the serious turn the conversation had just taken.

"I brought pie," Phillip said after Momma motioned him in. He put it down on the table before looking at me seriously for a moment. "Is it okay if I hug you?" he asked me intently.

"I'll be offended if you don't," I replied, stepping into his embrace.

He pulled back after a few moments. "You're too skinny."

"I haven't heard that much before in my life," I said with a smile. "I see you've gotten back on the exercise-and-diet train yourself." When he'd first decided to court my mother, Phillip had gone on a strict regimen of eating and exercising, but over time, he'd slackened it a bit, adding some of his previous paunch back. To my surprise, it was nearly gone again.

He patted his belly. "I decided it was time. How are you? Really?"

"I'm a-okay," I said, promising myself that if I could help it, I'd stop using the word *fine* for the foreseeable future. To too many people, it seemed to offer an invitation to probe a little deeper. I knew I couldn't keep the resolution, but at least for the moment I would try. "Are you two joining us for dinner?" I asked, surveying the massive array of food on my kitchen table. "You're more than welcome to, since there's clearly enough to feed a small army here."

"Thank you, but we've already eaten," Momma said. "Feel free to invite anyone you choose, though." She studied Grace for a moment before adding, "I'm sure your young man would appreciate a home-cooked meal, not that you don't provide him with any," she hastily added, backpedaling swiftly.

"Nothing like this, I'm afraid," Grace answered with a smile. "The police chief is at a law enforcement convention in Charlotte for the next four days."

"Who's minding the store in his absence?" Phillip asked, since he'd once held the office himself.

"Rick and Darby are taking turns," Grace said with a smile. "I'm not sure it's going so well. I hear they are having a bit of a power struggle at the moment."

"Maybe I should offer *my* services until the chief gets back," my stepfather said.

"Dear, we discussed this earlier."

"I know we did," Phillip said with a sigh. "Sometimes I just feel so useless."

"That's nonsense, and you know it. You're very important to me," Momma said.

"And as significant as that is to me, a man has to have a purpose, or what good is he?" Phillip glanced at Grace and me and suddenly realized we were intently following their conversation. "Sorry, ladies."

"Don't apologize," I said. "Jake and I have had that exact same conversation. Why do you think he's off working another freelance gig right now?"

"Do you think I might be able to tag along next time?" Phillip asked eagerly.

I didn't have to even glance Momma's way to see that she wasn't in favor of the idea at all, but it wasn't my place to kill the man's dreams. "You'll have to talk to Jake about it," I said.

"Then that's what I'll do," he said. I swear he seemed to brighten up a bit just at the mere thought of doing serious work again. "Thanks, Suzanne."

"Don't thank me. I literally didn't do anything."

"Maybe not, but you didn't kill it out of hand, either." He turned to his wife and kissed her cheek. "I'll go wait out in the car while you tell Suzanne what a terrible idea this is."

He was laughing as he left. When I turned to Momma, I expected to find her scowling, but to my surprise, she looked pensive. "He has a point, doesn't he? People need to feel useful."

"Momma, I don't think there's one chance in a hundred that Jake will let Phillip join him. He's working with some pretty heavy hitters."

"Are you implying that my husband isn't good enough?" Momma asked me frostily.

"Nothing of the sort," I said. "If I ask him nicely, Jake might be able to work something out."

"Well, let's not go that far," Momma said, her frown turning into a smile. "Don't worry about Phillip. We'll figure something

out. Now, you two ladies enjoy your meal and the rest of your evening. Any plans in particular?"

"I'm not sure. Maybe another movie?" I asked as I looked at Grace hopefully.

"I'm all up for a triple-header if you are," she said with a grin.

"Then it's settled," I said. I hugged my mother, and Grace joined in on the other side. The sandwich of bodies we made nearly made Momma disappear. Only her laughter gave her away. "Will you two kindly unhand me?" she asked happily.

"We just want you to know how much we appreciate you feeding us dinner," I said.

"And the pie, too. Don't forget the pie," Grace added.

"For as long as you've known me, have you *ever* known of a time where I forgot there was pie?" I asked as we freed Momma from our joint embrace.

"No, that's a fair point," Grace said. "Just in case though, maybe we should start our meal with a slice each."

Momma started to say something and then just as quickly bit it back.

"Something you wanted to add, Momma?" I asked her.

"No, not at all. Enjoy your meal and the rest of your evening. I love both of you scamps very much."

"And we love you just as much, if not more," I said.

"That, my dear sweet child, is impossible," Momma answered with a nod.

After they were gone, Grace looked at me. "I was dead serious about eating pie first."

"Do I look as though I have a problem with that?" I asked her with a grin.

The meal was spectacular, especially since we bookended the main course with pie as an appetizer and more pie for dessert. Grace pushed back from the table when we finished. "I don't think I could eat another bite."

"Me, either. After we put the leftovers away, I want to change my vote from a movie to a nap."

"I'm game if you are, but don't you have to go to bed soon anyway?"

"Not for hours and hours," I said as I glanced at the clock on the wall. "Well, at least one hour."

"That means there's no time for a movie, but I have another idea."

"As long as I don't have to leave the house, I'm willing to consider it," I said.

"Let's see what Annabeth painted you," she said as she stretched. "Can you bring yourself to do it yet?"

"I suppose so," I said. "Before we do though, can we have coffee and sit on the couch for a few minutes?"

"Sure. Are you really that stuffed?"

"I'm full, if that's what you're asking, but I'd like to spend a little time remembering Annabeth before we peek at the painting she did for me. I didn't get to go to the funeral, so I'd kind of like to say good-bye in my own way. Is that silly of me?"

"Not at all," Grace replied. "I think Annabeth would have appreciated the gesture."

We both grabbed mugs of coffee and headed into the living room. The fire was starting to die down, so I poked it a bit and added another log. Grace had been right. I needed to get to bed soon, but if we were going to open Annabeth's painting, I wanted a chance to say good-bye to her properly first, and the only way I knew to do that was to remember the good times we'd shared together. It was the only service I wanted for her, so it was fitting that we were doing it for my lost friend.

CHAPTER 4

"**D**o you want to start with the first story, or should I?" Grace asked me once we were settled in in front of the fire.

"I will," I said. "Remember the time in art class we all got thrown out?"

"You'll have to be more specific than that," Grace answered with a smile. "As I recall, it happened on more than one occasion."

"I'm talking about when we drew caricatures of Mr. Brimbsy."

"Oh, yes. I still say we would have gotten away with it if Annabeth hadn't been so good at it. You couldn't tell from *our* sketches who it was, but she nailed his hooked nose perfectly. I wonder what ever happened to that drawing?"

"Hang on a second," I said as I headed toward the new closet that Jake had built under the stairs during his period of boredom after retirement the year before. He hadn't wanted to build an ordinary closet. No, my husband had seen something online about disguising its presence completely, and even I had to admit that if I hadn't known it was there, I never would have been able to find it. Using the magnetic catch in the drawer of the table beside it, I slid it in place, and voilà, the door opened as if by magic.

"What are you doing?" she asked me curiously.

"Just give me a minute." I went digging through one of the boxes of my memories and soon found what I was looking for. "Is that what you were talking about?" I asked her with a grin as

I presented her with the exact same drawing Annabeth had done a lifetime ago.

"How did you get your hands on this?" she asked as she pulled out her phone and took a photo of it. "I thought old Brimsby destroyed the evidence."

"It was in Annabeth's permanent file, at least for a few days. I worked in the office as a volunteer that year, remember?"

"Are you telling me that you actually stole it from her file?" Grace asked me incredulously.

"You don't think less of me, do you?"

"You're kidding, right? I have literally never been more proud to call you my friend than I am at this very moment," she said. "I bet old man Brimsby was livid when he found out who did it."

"I'm not sure that he ever did," I admitted. "We both thought of him as old back then, didn't we?"

"He had to be at least sixty," Grace admitted.

"I was doing a little surfing online, and I looked up some of our old teachers. He was a year younger than we are now when we had him in class."

"That is impossible," Grace said.

"I can show you the proof if you don't believe me."

"No, I trust you. I'm just having a hard time wrapping my head around it."

"I checked three different sources, and they all agreed. It's amazing how your definition of 'young' changes as you get older, isn't it?"

"No doubt." She studied the image again. "She even included a few symbols we used in our secret code. What does it say? Can you still read it?"

I studied it for a few moments, but I couldn't recall what the code said off the top of my head. "I have a key code somewhere in my things. It was clever of us making up a written language that only the three of us could read."

Grace pointed to one corner of the drawing. "Hang on a second. This is signed by the artist. I don't remember us signing our work back then."

"We didn't. I offered it to Annabeth as soon as I stole it, but she refused. She said that since I took the risk, I deserved the reward. When she signed it with a flourish, she said, 'Keep it. You have my permission to sell it when I'm dead, but don't wait too long.' It was a little too prescient for my taste, though we both laughed it off back then."

"You're not really going to sell anything she did for you, are you?" Grace asked.

"I wouldn't part with a single thing, no matter how much it might be worth. To me, it's all priceless."

"So let's open the painting already," Grace said. "I'm dying to see it."

I stifled a massive yawn, not realizing how much coming home would take out of me. "Sure thing. Let me get my scissors."

Grace put a hand on mine. "You know what? It can wait. You need to get to bed, young lady."

I glanced at the clock. "But it's still early, even for me."

"Most days, I would agree, but your system has had quite a few shocks today. Tell me the truth, Suzanne. If I left right now, how long would it take you to fall asleep? And don't even think about lying to me, woman."

"I suppose I might last another ten minutes," I admitted.

"That's all I needed to know." Grace stood, and when I followed suit, she hugged me again. "Let's open it tomorrow after you're finished working, if you're up for it then."

"Okay. It's a deal," I said, suddenly feeling a wave of weariness wash over me. Coming back home was just part of it. Jake leaving so soon was another part. But the biggest reason I was exhausted was learning that I'd lost a friend.

"I'll come by at eleven tomorrow. That is, if you're sure you

don't want me to go in with you in the morning," she offered again.

"It's sweet of you to offer, but I'll be fine."

"Then I won't push you about it." Grace put on her heavy jacket and a lovely scarf I hadn't seen before. "Is that new?"

"It is. It's straight from Ireland. I decided I needed a little treat."

I couldn't imagine how much it must have cost, more than I made in a week at the donut shop no doubt, but I wasn't envious of my friend. I'd chosen the exact life I needed, and I knew that I wouldn't be any happier if I had more money. Well, maybe a little happier, I thought with a smile.

"What's so funny?" Grace asked.

"I'm just glad to be home," I said, deflecting the real question.

"I'm just as pleased about that myself," she said.

After Grace was gone, I went straight to bed, but sleep wouldn't come, despite what I'd told her. Finally, I couldn't take it anymore, so I got up and moved back into the living room. As I did, I passed the painting Annabeth had so graciously created for me. I was pleased to have something so recently from her, but at the moment, it just made me sad. Jake's secret closet was still open, so I slid it inside and closed the door. Maybe if it were out of sight, it would be out of mind, as the old adage went.

Before curling up on the couch with a quilt, I put a few more logs on the fire. There was something mesmerizing about it that knocked me out faster than a sleeping pill could have.

When I woke up to the sound of the alarm on my phone, I roused myself and started getting ready for work.

I was about to start over again in many ways, and I was ready for a fresh set of challenges.

It was time to stop focusing on myself, and my recovery, and bring sweet treats to the world again.

As I made the short drive to the donut shop in the frigid darkness, I wondered how it would feel being back in a place I loved so much but had endured such a bad thing in so recently. I'd come close to dying there, and only a fluke of luck had saved me from my attacker. It had happened months ago, but I still felt my anxiety grow more and more as I approached the shop. I wasn't sure exactly what I was expecting when I pulled up in front of Donut Hearts, but it certainly wasn't discovering the lights already blazing inside and two people sitting at the counter in the front of the shop waiting for me.

"I wasn't expecting to find you two here this morning," I said as I pulled off my gloves, hat, scarf, and jacket. The temperature had dropped since the night before, but that's what happened in January in our part of North Carolina. It wouldn't have surprised me if I'd seen snow coming down on the way in, but that hadn't happened. I looked from my assistant, Emma, to her mother, Sharon. "What's going on?"

"Suzanne, we need to talk," Emma said, looking a bit grim.

"Okay. I'm listening," I said. What was going on here? Was this some kind of intervention?

"First things first," Emma said as she hugged me with great vigor. "I'm so glad you're back."

I hugged her a few moments longer, then broke free from her embrace. "I was beginning to worry about that. You two looked so serious, I wasn't at all sure that you were all that happy to see me."

"Nonsense," Sharon said as she stepped forward. "Give me my turn, Emma."

Her daughter did as she suggested, and Sharon gave me a briefer, though no less sincere, hug of her own. "How are you, dear?"

"I'm okay," I said, looking around. "Did you paint in here?" I asked, noticing that the color of the walls was a few shades darker than it had been before.

"I hope you don't mind," Emma said. "We thought it could use a little freshening up. If you hate it, we'll be happy to repaint it ourselves."

"No, I like it," I said. It was close to my original color yet somehow different enough to give the place a new vibe.

"I'm so glad," Emma said, clearly relieved.

"That's not why you two were here waiting to ambush me, was it?" I asked them.

"Oh, dear. We didn't mean to do that. It's just that there's something we need to discuss, and we need to do it before you get started with your work today."

"Let me just turn the fryer on, make some coffee, and then we can chat," I said.

"The fryer's already on, and the coffee's ready," Emma said, pouring me a mug.

"Okay," I said as I took a sip. It was a bit stronger than I normally liked, but coffee had always been part of Emma's domain. "Shoot."

"We've been discussing our earlier arrangement with you, and we're not satisfied with it," Emma said.

Her announcement shocked me, and if I were being honest about it, it hurt a little, too. "I'm not sure how much *more* I can give you than all of the profits you've made since I've been gone. What did you have in mind?"

"That's just it," Sharon said. "You were too generous, and we took advantage of you."

"Nonsense. It was only fair," I protested. "You two put in *all* of the work over the past two months. I wasn't even around to help out."

"But you put up the original capital investment that bought this business," Sharon countered. "The way we see it, the profits should be split into thirds." She pushed a stack of deposit slips toward me, neatly banded together. As I riffled through them, I saw that they'd been making regular deposits the entire time Jake and I had been gone. "This isn't fair, as much as I appreciate the sentiment."

"We could give you half, if that would suit you better," Emma said with a grin.

"That's not it, and you know it. It's too much as it is," I protested.

"Suzanne, Mom and I have discussed this, and it's not up for debate. Either you take your share of the profits while you were gone, or we're going to have a real problem," Emma said.

"Well, I don't want any problems," I said as I glanced at the total amount, thoughtfully provided on a sticky note included with the slips. "This is awfully generous of you both."

Sharon smiled. "We wouldn't have it any other way. Besides, you've already financed my next four trips, so I should be the one thanking you."

"And I made quite a bit more than I would have as a wage slave," Emma added with a wicked little grin of her own. "We *all* come out ahead."

"Thank you. Both of you," I said as I hugged them each in turn again. "Did anything exciting happen while I was away?"

Emma and Sharon shared a quick glance, and I knew that something was up.

"Not really," Emma said a little haltingly.

"Emma," I scolded her, much in the tone that a mother would use with her misbehaving child.

"Tell her," Sharon said. "If you don't, I will."

"Someone tried to break into the donut shop a few days ago," Emma confessed. "It was most likely just some kids."

I looked around my shop, horrified that it had been violated yet again. "Did they do much damage?"

"That's the thing. As far as we could tell, nothing was taken," Emma said. "George paid a locksmith from Union Square to come fix the lock, and we were even able to get him to reset it using your old key. You know how these things are, Suzanne. We didn't want to worry you."

"Well, if you're sure nothing was taken," I said.

"Unless you had a thousand dollars tucked into a dark corner that I didn't know about, we're good," Emma said with a shrug.

"Okay then," I said, knowing that things happened, whether I was in town or not. "Is that all that happened?"

"That's it. I promise," Emma said.

"Good enough. Thanks again for splitting the profits with me. I can't tell you how much I appreciate it," I said as I tapped the stack of deposit slips. I certainly didn't want them to think that I held the break-in against them, especially since nothing had been taken. What was important to me was that they knew that their generosity meant more to me than the money, though it would certainly come in handy. "You know, you both didn't have to get up quite so early for this conversation," I said. "I figured you would want to sleep in."

"The truth is, I'm getting used to the hours, and Emma has been doing it with you all along," Sharon said. "Besides, we thought you might like some company your first day back. We're ready and waiting to pitch in. All you have to do is say the word, and we'll get busy."

I didn't know how I could graciously refuse their offer, but

every time I'd imagined this moment during my recovery, I'd done it alone, and somehow, that was what I needed. "Would I be totally ungrateful if I thanked you, but said 'no thanks'?" I asked them softly.

"Of course not," Emma said, patting my shoulder. "Whatever makes it easier for you is what we want. I get wanting to solo this morning on your first day back. Come on, Mom, let me buy your breakfast."

"It's much too early to eat," Sharon said.

"Speak for yourself, John Alden," she said with a grin. As they girded themselves up for the cold, Emma said, "If you change your mind, I'm just a phone call away."

"Thanks for everything," I said as I walked them out the front door. "I can't tell you how much it meant to me knowing that the shop was in such good hands."

"It was our pleasure," Emma said, and her mother nodded in agreement.

"Welcome back, Suzanne," Sharon said.

"We missed you," Emma added.

"I missed you, too," I said.

Once they were gone, I took a deep breath, and then I walked back into the kitchen where the last assault had originated. Emma and Sharon had rearranged things to their liking, but it took only a few minutes to get things back to my layout. There wasn't anything wrong with what they'd done; it just wasn't my way. I was glad they'd left things the way they'd been while I was gone. Moving the tools of my trade back to their rightful places gave me a sense of ownership of the space again. Soon I was churning out cake donuts again, back where I belonged at last.

CHAPTER 5

"Wow, I never expected to find a crowd out front waiting for me to open my doors," I said as I saw that a great many of my dearest friends and oldest customers were waiting for me to open Donut Hearts when six a.m. rolled around. Making the donuts had been therapeutic for me, but seeing everyone waiting to see me was almost more than my heart could stand.

"George, it's so good to see you," I said as I stood by the door and welcomed our mayor, and one of my best friends, inside first.

"Suzanne, you're looking well," he said.

"Have you lost weight, Mr. Mayor?" I asked him.

"Nothing like you have," he countered. "You're practically wasting away, young lady."

"I'm sure it's a temporary state of being," I answered with a smile. "It's tough keeping the pounds off in my line of work."

"I'm just so happy you came back to continue it," George said.

"Was there ever any doubt in your mind?" I asked him.

"*I* knew you'd come back to us, but a few folks around town were beginning to wonder," the mayor admitted.

"April Springs is my home, no matter what," I said, believing it to be true with all of my heart. After all, if an attempted homicide or two hadn't been able to drive me away, what would? "Can I get you something?"

"A dozen old-fashioned donuts and a cup of coffee," he said. "Will that be for here?" I asked him with a grin. I knew that the mayor enjoyed my treats, but usually one or two at a time.

"Sadly, no. I have a meeting this morning I have to prep for," he said, "and I thought your goodies might help pave the way for some kind of accord."

I got him his treats to go, and after returning his change, I added, "You're becoming more and more like a statesman every day."

"Take that back," he said with the hint of a smile. Our mayor had certainly grown into his job, especially given how he'd been when he'd first been elected.

"If that's all you're getting, Mr. Mayor, the rest of us are patiently waiting our turns," Angelica DeAngelis said behind him. "After all, we've got a restaurant to open."

"By all means, ladies," George said as he stepped aside, smiling broadly at her as he did so. Not only was Angelica there to see me, but so were all four of her daughters, each more beautiful than the last, but none of them able to hold a candle to their mother.

"Hey, ladies," I said as I smiled at Antonia, Maria, Tianna, and Sophia. "I can't believe she let you *all* come."

"She really didn't have much choice. If she hadn't, we were going to all go out on strike," Sophia said with a grin.

Maria said, "Sophia, we agreed to be positive for Suzanne."

"How much more positive can I be than to tell her we were willing to lose our wages if it meant not being able to see her?" Sophia asked.

I didn't want the DeAngelis women clashing in my store, even if it was all generated from the love they clearly had for each other. "What will it be, ladies?"

"Two dozen donuts to go, your choice," Sophia said, and then she glanced at her mother for confirmation of her order.

"Suzanne, I'm afraid my daughter misspoke," Angelica said.

"Mother, we agreed," Sophia said sharply.

"I'm sorry, but I'm overruling you all and making an executive decision." She turned to me and added, "There are five of us. We would like five dozen donuts, please."

"Score," Sophia said with a smile. "Way to go, Mom!"

"What on earth are you going to do with five dozen donuts?" I asked her, laughing as I did so.

"If any of them make it through the drive back to Union Square, they are going to be on the dessert menu today," she said. "We wanted to be here to welcome you back, Suzanne. You've been sorely missed."

I knew better than to argue with Angelica, so as I started boxing up the donuts, I turned to her for a moment and smiled. "I missed you all, too."

"When are you going to come see us?" Tianna asked. "And don't forget to bring that handsome husband of yours."

"Soon, I hope," I said, not wanting to get into Jake's absence at the moment.

"Ladies, Napoli's awaits," Angelica said as each woman took a box of donuts with her. I tried to give her a friends-and-family discount, but Angelica was too quick for me. "I'm paying the full price, Suzanne."

"Then I'm paying the menu prices at Napoli's from now on, too," I said just as directly.

Angelica wavered for a moment, but then she finally relented. "Very well."

Sophia looked at her mother worriedly. "Are you feeling okay, Mom?"

"I'm fine," Angelica said curtly. "Why do you ask?"

"I've just never seen you back down before," her daughter said with a smile.

All the matriarch could do was laugh, a sound that warmed me throughout.

Once the DeAngelis women were gone, I could swear the place lost a bit of its light.

Over the next three hours, there was a parade of old friends and regular customers, including, but not limited to: Paige Hill, the bookstore owner; chef extraordinaire Barton Gleason; For the Birds owner, Jenny Preston; Trish Granger, owner of the Boxcar Grill; and many more. It somehow felt as though it was my birthday, only everyone was buying donuts, too. I was nearly out of inventory by nine a.m. when the crowd finally slackened off. To my surprise, Alyssa Winchell, Annabeth's mother, started to come in. Her hand was actually on the door, but then she changed her mind at the last second and headed off down the street. I wanted to stop her, but I was the only one working in the shop. Maybe I shouldn't have sent Emma home after all. I was going to have to look Alyssa up later. I wanted to express my condolences for the loss of her daughter in person.

I was pulled from my thoughts by someone else approaching, a friend in the broadest sense of the word, and one whose presence in my life was still a constant source of surprise to me.

"Hi, Gabby. I'm afraid if you've come by the shop for donuts, my selection is pretty limited at the moment."

My business neighbor, owner and proprietress of the upscale used clothing store ReNEWed, frowned at me, her usual expression when she looked in my direction. "Suzanne, it appears in your absence that you've lost the ability to gauge your customers' interest in your product line," Gabby said a bit stiffly, though I knew that she was happy to see me as well.

"Actually, I got a little carried away and made more than I thought I'd need. I just wasn't expecting such a big turnout."

"Give them time," she said dryly. "The tide will trickle away soon enough."

I wasn't about to let her dampen my mood. "If you're not here for donuts, to what do I owe the pleasure of your company?"

"It's about this," she said as she thrust a flyer into my hands. "STOP CRIME IN APRIL SPRINGS," the banner said.

Below it, I read a recap of the break-in at my shop, highly dramatized, and a few other clearly random acts of vandalism. At the very bottom, in bold letters again, the flyer ended, "JOIN BUSINESSES UNITED TOGETHER."

"BUT?" I asked her.

"But what? Suzanne, you were a victim, whether you knew it or not at the time. I can't believe that you of all people would hesitate in joining my efforts to keep this town safe."

"BUT," I repeated.

"But what?" she asked, clearly growing more and more irritated with me.

"The acronym for your committee spells out B.U.T.," I told her, doing my best to suppress my grin but just as clearly failing miserably at it.

"Honestly, are you ever going to grow up?"

"I sincerely hope not," I told her. "Gabby, Emma and Sharon told me that it was probably just some random kids."

"And that justifies vandalism in your mind?" she asked me archly.

"No, of course not, but I trust the police chief."

"I might as well, if he were actually here, but instead, we have two police officers that together fail to equal a tenth of their supervisor's ability."

"Is that a compliment you are paying Stephen Grant?" Gabby had been rather vocal about our young police chief's lack of experience in the past, so this was a surprise to me.

"No," she said emphatically. "It just shows how much *less* I think of his successors."

"They *are* temporary," I reminded her. "The chief will be back next week."

"We'll be lucky if any of our shops are still standing by then," she said.

There was only one way I was going to get rid of Gabby. "I'd be honored to join up. What do I have to do?"

Gabby smiled smugly as she handed me the flyer she'd been waving around earlier. "Put this in your window, and keep an eye out on what's happening in front of your shop on Springs Drive."

Those were two easy enough things to promise her. "Done and done," I said.

Gabby nodded her approval, and then she started for the door before she pivoted. When she looked at me again, I saw that her hardened expression had softened quite a bit. "It really is good to have you back. I missed you, Suzanne."

"I missed you too, Gabby," I said, startling myself even as I'd said the words. It was true, in fact. Gabby was a part of April Springs, not necessarily always a lovely part, but a part of my life all the same.

I sold my last donut at twenty minutes after nine. I knew that it was a good hour and forty minutes before I was due to close Donut Hearts, but not only was I completely out of inventory thanks to my friends and loyal customers, I was also exhausted. I was not used to making donuts and running the shop, let alone by myself, but there was an emotional toll the day had taken as well. I flipped the sign from OPEN to CLOSED and set about shutting the place down for the day. In twenty minutes the register balanced, the place was clean as a whistle, and I needed a nap, badly. After dropping off my deposit at the bank, one of

the best financial days I'd ever had at Donut Hearts, I headed home for some much-needed rest.

When I got there, though, a shot of adrenaline hit me. Someone was trying to break in through my front door, at least that was what it looked like to me! I blew the Jeep horn as I skidded around the corner, and whovever was there took off like a shot into the woods beside the cottage. There were many advantages to owning a place on the edge of a park, but visibility was not one of them. Whoever had been trying to get in had been wearing black sweats and a hoodie sweatshirt pulled down over their face. I couldn't even swear if it was a man or a woman. I slammed the Jeep into my spot and got out, ready to pursue whoever had just been trying to pay me an unlawful visit.

Then I heard a familiar voice behind me.

"Grace, did you see that?" I asked her as I started to pursue my potential robber around the side of my cottage.

"See what?" she asked as she joined in the chase. I loved that about her, that she was willing to risk life and limb simply on my say-so.

"Someone was trying to break into the cottage just now," I said as I looked around the park. The morning was still bitterly cold, which was appropriate weather for early in the year, but that meant that there were no witnesses to see who exactly might have been fleeing my premises. One thing was certain: whoever it had been was long gone now.

She looked around the empty park. "I don't see anybody."

"Neither do I, but *someone* was there," I told her.

"I believe you, but whoever it was is long gone now. What could they have wanted?"

"I have no idea," I admitted as we walked back to the house. After examining the lock and the frame around it, I said, "There are no signs of anyone trying to break in."

"Is it possible they were just here to see you?" Grace asked me.

"Maybe, but if that was the case, why did they run when I came around the corner?" I asked her.

"Well, you were driving like a madwoman, and you were blowing your horn like crazy, too," Grace said. "Maybe you frightened them off."

"*Me? They* scared the daylights out of *me*," I said as I let us both inside.

"Are you going to call the police?" Grace asked me.

I thought about it for a few seconds before shaking my head. "If Stephen were here, I probably would, but with Rick and Darby at the helm, I'm not sure I want to go through that."

"I get that," Grace said. "If we just had some evidence, besides your word, I mean, it might be different."

"It does sound a little crazy, doesn't it?" I conceded. "Why would anyone want to break in here? The donut shop I understand; to someone uninformed, they might think there was the possibility of finding money there, but here?"

"Hang on a second," Grace said. "Someone tried to break into Donut Hearts, too?"

"Evidently. Emma and Sharon told me it was probably just vandals. Hey, what are you doing?"

"I'm calling Rick and Darby," she said. "One break-in I'm willing to swallow, but two?"

I didn't even fight her on it.

She was probably right. Maybe it was time to bring the police in on this before things got even worse.

CHAPTER 6

"**I**T WAS PROBABLY THOSE KIDS in Hudson Creek again," Rick said after looking around the place. "We heard about the donut shop, and it sounded like their doing, too."

Not to be outdone, Darby said, "They've been breaking into places and taking selfies for their photomat pages."

"That's not what it's called," Rick said.

"Who cares? The point is, it's just vandalism, pure and simple."

"Probably," Rick conceded.

"Hang on. That might explain the donut shop, but why would they hit Suzanne's place?" Grace asked.

"Maybe they are stepping up their game," Darby said.

"It's possible," Rick agreed.

"The real question is, what are you two going to do about it?" Grace asked them as though she were their elementary school teacher.

"We'll step up the patrols out here," Rick said.

"That sounds good," Darby agreed.

"Do I need to call your boss?" she asked them in a scolding tone.

"There's no need to bring the chief in on this," Rick said plaintively.

"Yeah, there's nothing he'd be able to do that we aren't planning anyway. Do us a favor. Don't call him, Grace."

Both men looked so uncomfortable by the prospect of having their boss brought in that I couldn't bear being the cause of it. "Just keep your eyes open and we won't call anyone yet," I said. "I doubt whoever it was will come back after the way I scared them off, anyway."

"You should have called us first thing when you saw them trying to break in," Darby scolded me.

"If I'd waited for you, they would have already been inside," I countered.

"That's not fair. After all, we got here two minutes after you called," Rick reminded me.

I couldn't disagree with him, but it had still been time enough for whoever it was to get in and out again, if they knew what they were looking for. What could that have been, though?

"If there's nothing else, we have a meeting with the mayor in ten minutes," Rick said as he glanced at his watch.

"Yeah, he's trying to give us advice we don't need and haven't asked for."

"Is he the *only* one doing that?" I asked, suddenly feeling sorry for the pair.

"No, your stepfather has been pretty vocal about pitching in, too. I don't suppose there's any chance you wouldn't mention this to him, is there?"

"Not a single one in the world," I said. After offering a slight smile, I added, "Sorry about that, but family comes first."

"I get that," Rick said as he headed for the door. "Bye, Suzanne."

"Call us if anything else happens," Darby added.

"You bet," I said, thanking them for coming.

——————◄◦►——————

"A fat lot of good that did," Grace said. "I have half a mind to call Stephen and tell him to cut his convention short. We need him back here."

"Grace, we might not like it, but they were right. What could Chief Grant do that they haven't already promised to do? Let's just leave it alone and see what happens."

"Okay, but I want to go on record saying that I don't like it."

"Duly noted," I said with a smile.

"You're back home early," Grace said after we settled down on the couch.

"My friends and loyal customers bought me out," I said. "The DeAngelis clan even came by in full force."

"Wow, that must have been something to see."

"Watching them walk out with five dozen donuts was the real sight. It was the best advertising I could have ever asked for," I said.

"I bet. So, how was it being back at the helm? Did you see any ghosts?"

I knew what Grace meant, at least I think I did. She wasn't literally talking about spirits from beyond but specters from my past, including the most recent one. "I had a few queasy moments, but in the end, it was just like being back home again," I told her. "I desperately needed that."

"I bet you did. So, what would you like to do today? That is if you have enough energy to do anything."

"I thought I needed a nap before, but now I'm feeling pretty good. You don't have to babysit me, you know."

"I understand that I don't *have* to," Grace said with a grin, "but I *want* to. As a matter of fact, I can't think of a better way of spending some of my vacation time than hanging out with you."

"Then you are showing a severe lack of imagination," I said with a grin. "But the truth is, that sounds great to me. First things first, though. Let's see that painting." I hadn't been able to stop thinking about it all morning at my shop, and I knew that I was ready at last to see what Annabeth had painted for

me. After Grace and I opened it, I was going to suggest we go see Alyssa to tell Annabeth's mother just how much her daughter had meant to me.

"I thought you'd never get around to it," Grace said with a grin. "Do you want to get it, or should I?"

"I'll grab it," I said. "You don't know the combination."

"Are you telling me that there's an actual lock on the door?" Grace asked as she followed me to the closet under the stairs.

"Kind of," I said as I retrieved the magnet that sprang the lock. After showing her how it was done, I stepped in and took out the painting. It was about the size of a coffee-table book but not nearly as thick. Even though it was wrapped in plain brown paper, I still took pains to open it gently. After all, I didn't want to take a chance and damage the painting beneath it.

Grace was more of a tear-your-way-in kind of gal. "Come on, Suzanne. It's just plain old butcher's paper."

"Patience is a virtue," I told her as I stuck my tongue out at her.

"Well, nobody in their right mind has *ever* accused me of being a virtuous woman," she said with a grin.

As I began to pull the paper off slowly, something fluttered to the floor. "I wonder what that is?" I asked as I bent down to pick it up.

"I haven't seen any of this before either, remember?" she asked me.

The sheet had some scribbling on it, but no ordinary person would be able to make out the symbols.

Then again, they hadn't created a code in school like the three of us had a very long time ago.

———◦❰❍❱◦———

I grabbed the notebook I had used the night before and flipped it to the key code. "Grab a pad from the kitchen and write this down," I told Grace.

She did as I asked, and I started reading aloud as I matched up the symbols of our homemade code with the letters we'd attached them to so long ago.

)$$%*&**(()++!!$#@^&&^$... and on and on.

"What does it say?" I asked Grace as I flipped the sheet over to make sure there was nothing on the back.

HELP ME, PLEASE! SOMEONE IS TRYING TO KILL ME!

"That's it? That's all that it says?" I asked Grace.

"You read me the symbols. All I did was write down what you told me."

"There's got to be more to it than that," I said. "Who would want to kill Annabeth? She was one of the sweetest people I knew."

"You'd be surprised. After all, we all manage to pick up a few enemies along the way, especially the more successful we get in life," Grace said.

"Thoughts like that make me happy I'm such a nobody," I said in all sincerity.

"You're not a nobody to me," she said. "What is the painting of, anyway?"

"I never got that far. Let's see," I said as I finished unwrapping the paper. Grace was still staring at the urgent note Annabeth had left me in code when I said, "Come over here and check this out."

"What is it, a cow? I'd love to see her rendition of a farm animal. No, it's probably some wild-looking donut, isn't it?"

"It's not the painting I want you to see," I said as I started to smooth out the wrinkled brown butcher's paper. Inside, on the interior part that had faced the painting—which I still hadn't seen—was a series of scrawls, notes, and more code, all in Annabeth's all-too-familiar handwriting. "What do you make of it?"

"Is it possible she lost her mind there toward the end?" Grace asked me gently. "Most of this is just pure nonsense."

"Grace, I spoke with her just before I left town, and she was perfectly sane then," I said.

"I know. It's as though she's put all of her scattered thoughts down on this paper, but why did she use it to wrap your gift?"

"Don't you see? These aren't random at all. I'm willing to bet my life on it. Somewhere in this jumble, Annabeth was trying to tell us who wanted to kill her. Now it's up to us to figure it out and bring her murderer to justice."

"She died from an accident, Suzanne. Remember?"

"Was it, though? Really? How do we know it wasn't staged to look that way? What if whoever killed her wanted the world to think that it was purely accidental?"

"I don't know," Grace said, clearly troubled. "Everyone just assumed that she fell off the ladder and hit her head on the side of her work table. Stephen seemed to be sure of it." It was clear that she didn't want anything to reflect badly on her boyfriend, but we couldn't ignore the facts. Still, I didn't have to beat her over the head with it.

"Grace, Stephen thought it was an accident because he didn't have all of the facts we do. If Annabeth hadn't left us this hodgepodge of information and a note to tell us what she suspected might happen to her, we would have accepted it, too."

"That's true," Grace said. "We need to figure out what she was trying to tell us and then see if we can find her killer ourselves."

"Should we tell Rick and Darby what we've discovered?" I asked, though it was the last thing I wanted to do. Annabeth had entrusted this to me, and I meant to see it through.

"I don't think there's any reason to alert *anyone* just yet," Grace said. "After all, we're assuming that Annabeth was right

and not just being paranoid. Let's dig into this a little deeper, and then we can decide what we're going to do about it."

I looked at her steadily before I spoke again. "Is there any doubt in your mind that we're going to try to find the person who killed our friend?" I asked her.

"Not a chance in the world," Grace said with stiff resolve.

"Then grab that paper and let's get started," I said. Almost as an afterthought, I flipped the painting over and looked to see what she'd painted for me.

The canvas was blank!

It was clear that the message on the butcher paper was what was important, but I was still a little disappointed that I wouldn't get one last painting from my late friend.

CHAPTER 7

"WHY IS IT BLANK?" GRACE asked as she looked over my shoulder.

"It's got to be a message to focus on the paper," I said.

"Wow, she really was worried about her life to send you a blank canvas just to share her worries with you."

I grabbed the blank canvas and stuck it back into Jake's closet, since that seemed to be the handiest place for it.

When I got back to the dining room, Grace was taking lots of photos of the wrapping paper or, more importantly, Annabeth's random notes written on it. "I thought it might be helpful to have a record of this," she said.

"I'm all for it. Let's take our photos, and then we can start digging into what she was trying to tell us," I answered as I pulled my cell phone back out and began taking photos of my own.

"If you don't mind," I said as I finished my last picture, "I'd like to leave the original out and work from that. When we're ready to go, we can stuff it into Jake's closet."

"I was about to suggest that very thing," Grace said with a grin. "Once again, great minds think alike."

"And they don't come any greater than ours," I said, and a moment later, we both burst out laughing from the sheer lunacy of my joke. "I'm not even sure where to start," I said in wonder as I stared at the jumbled mess. There were bubbles with names

in them connected via a line network that would have made a cartographer proud.

"What's the difference between a bubble and a box?" Grace asked as she pointed to different parts of the sheet.

"I'm not sure there is one, but we should probably take note of what is in what, just in case it's significant. Are they bubbles or circles? Boxes or squares?"

"I'm not sure what we call them is significant. Shall you decipher and I record our notes?" she asked.

"If you don't mind," I said. "Let's start at the top left-hand corner."

"Is there any reason in particular why?" she asked me.

"I don't know. It just seems as good a place as any," I answered truthfully.

"Hey, that works for me," Grace said.

The first bubble had Annabeth's mother's name inside it. "'Alyssa Winchell,'" I announced, "is written inside a bubble."

"Surely you don't think her mother killed her," Grace said, clearly aghast at the very thought of it.

"I'm not thinking anything just yet," I said. "It's way too soon to try to get into Annabeth's head. I just want to see what we can come up with by breaking this down first."

"Okay, I can see that. Is her bubble connected to anything?"

I traced the lines that came off the bubble and found two more bubbles, one that surprised me. "Max is on here," I said.

"Your Max?" Grace asked me curiously.

"He hasn't been 'My Max' for a very long time," I said. "I suppose if he belongs to anyone these days, it's Emily Hargraves."

"You know what I meant," Grace said.

"Yes, it's Max, for sure. He's in a bubble, so maybe that's a good thing."

"Maybe," Grace said as she took note of it. "Any other bubbles connected to Alyssa?"

"Yes, but it's a name I'm not familiar with. 'Kerry Minter.' Does that name ring any bells?"

"No, but then again, Annabeth and I had drifted apart over the years."

"Well, we've stayed in touch," I said, "and that name is news to me."

"Let's put her on another list," Grace said as she flipped the page and wrote down the name. "Are there any leads from Max's bubble?"

"Just one that says 'Sarah Flowers.' What could that mean?"

"I haven't a clue," Grace said as she wrote it down. "Just out of curiosity, how many names are on that sheet?"

I took a few moments to count them. "Five are in bubbles, four are in squares," I said.

"Let's write all of the names down first, or will that wreck your system?" Grace asked.

"No, it's a good idea," I said. "Get ready. Let's start with bubbles and then move on to squares."

"I'm ready," she said.

"Okay, in the bubbles we've got Alyssa, Max, 'Kerry Minter,' 'Sarah Albright,' and mine."

The last one caught us both off guard. "*You* made the list, but *I* didn't? At least tell me I made it into a box," Grace asked.

"Nope, you aren't mentioned at all," I said. "Grace, that's not a bad thing. Why on earth did she put my name on this?"

"Are there any lines coming out from your name?" Grace asked as she leaned over my shoulder.

"It looks like a cracked windshield, there are so many of them," I admitted.

"Then it's solved. You did it, Suzanne. Come on, confess." She shook her head quickly. "That was in bad taste. Sorry, sometimes I go too far even for me. Maybe it means that you hold the answers to who killed her."

"If that was what she was counting on, I'm afraid she was wrong."

Grace touched my shoulder lightly. "Suzanne, it could mean that you were the only one she trusted enough to try to figure this out. That's what I think. The lines mean that you need to talk to all of the people listed here. Shall we go on to the box people now?"

"Is that what we're calling them?" I asked.

"It's as good a designation as any," she said.

"Okay, I guess you're right. The names in squares are 'Martin Lancaster,' 'Galen' (no last name), 'Christopho Langer,' and 'Bonnie Small.' I've never heard of *any* of these people."

"Me, either. Let's ask my friend," Grace said as she pulled out her phone.

"You have a friend who might know all of the answers?" I asked, wondering just how far a reach my best friend had.

"Sure. I bet you've heard of him. His name is Google."

I had to laugh. "Go on, see what you can find out."

After a few minutes, we had a rundown on all of the people we didn't know. It was my turn to take notes as Grace announced brief bios on all of our names. "Martin Lancaster owns a new gallery in Maple Hollow called Marcast; Galen, who incidentally doesn't use a last name, maybe she thinks she's Cher or somebody, is an artist who has had some unkind things to say about Annabeth's work; Christopho Langer is a fellow artist who seems to have nothing but praise for Annabeth's art; and then there's Bonnie Small. She represents all three artists and half a dozen others. According to this article, she's some kind of Southern art detector. Evidently she specializes in pulling artists out of obscurity and making them famous, at least on a regional basis."

"That's odd that all of the squares contain names from Annabeth's art world, while all of the bubbles are people she

knew personally, assuming Kerry Minter was a friend we just didn't know about."

"That's as good a theory as any, at least for now," Grace said. "What does that leave us?"

"Just these diamonds," I said. "Man, she wrote really small here, didn't she?"

"Do you need glasses?" Grace joked with me.

"No, I can see just fine, thank you very much." In the diamonds, there were what appeared to be events and locales, though what they meant was beyond me. Still, there were three of them, so I relayed the information to Grace. "We have: 'Marcast,' the art gallery Lancaster owns; 'Artie's,' the art supply warehouse in Union Square, and 'Studio,' which must be Annabeth's place."

"Okay, those are the places. What were the events?" Grace asked me.

"'Ladder?' is listed for her studio, 'Boxes?' is coupled with Artie's, and 'Car?' is with Marcast," I said. "What do you suppose they mean?"

"Near misses, I'm guessing," Grace said after studying the list.

"How do you get that?" I asked her.

"Well, let's say Annabeth was right. Someone was trying to kill her, or at least that's the way it felt to her. Her note didn't leave much room for doubt, did it? It just follows that those events were attempts on her life, at least as far as she was concerned."

"That all makes sense, but these diamonds don't have *any* lines radiating from them," I said, pointing out the paper trails.

"I never claimed to have *all* of the answers," my best friend said.

After a few moments of thought, I said, "Maybe she knew that the events were meant to kill her, but not who might be responsible for them."

"It makes sense to me. Is there anything else on the paper?" Grace asked me.

"Just some random numbers and more code, but they aren't associated with anything else."

"Decode the words and then we can figure out what they might mean," Grace said.

"Okay, here goes." As I read off the code letters and what they corresponded to in our ancient code book, I started putting the words together as it all came back to me. "Real, Not Real, Who? Why? Why Now? Money-Greed, Anger, Jealousy, Betrayal."

"So, now she's just listing random motives?" Grace asked. "Why did she feel the need to do that part of it in code?"

"Maybe she was just being paranoid," I said, remembering the painting she'd left me. "Look," I said as I held my face at an angle low to the paper. "She's erased some lines coming from these."

"Can you make out the direction they were going in?" Grace asked me.

"I might be wrong, but 'Greed' and 'Money' look as though they were both heading toward 'Bonnie Small,' and then one veered off toward 'Martin Lancaster,' but finally, she wiped the lines out altogether. 'Jealousy' could have been toward any of them, but 'Anger' is absolutely toward 'Galen.'"

"Okay, we'll have to see why she changed her mind about matching people with motives. In the meantime, what about the numbers? They are the last things we need to consider, right?"

"As far as I can tell," I said. "We've got '136,' '054,' '59,' and I'm not sure if this last one is '104' or '109.' I don't get what significance any of them have."

"I don't, either," Grace said, "but then again, we're just getting started." She stood and stretched. "I'm not sure what else we're going to get out of this right now. Do you need to rest before we go on?"

"No, I'm suddenly energized," I said.

"So, where should we start?"

"It has to be Annabeth's studio," I said. "I know it's in back of her old house, so it will give me a chance to speak with Alyssa while we're there."

"Then let's go," Grace said. She paused at the door and looked me over quickly. "You can change first."

"What's wrong with what I've got on?" I asked, glancing down at my normal wear, faded blue jeans and a T-shirt. Since it was chilly out, I'd added one of Jake's faded flannel shirts for two reasons. One was that it really did add another layer of warmth, but it also made me feel as though he was close by and not hundreds of miles away.

"The clothes are fine. It's the aroma that some folks might find questionable," she said with a grin. "I don't mean me, but some people."

I had already gotten used to the smell of donuts on my clothes and in my hair, and the truth was that I hadn't even noticed it. "Give me ten minutes and I'll be ready to roll."

"You're okay with me saying something about it, right?" she asked me tentatively.

"Hey, if your best friend can't tell you that you stink, who can?" I asked, laughing.

"That's not what I meant," Grace said, "but it's true enough."

"What, that I stink?" I asked with a smile.

"No, that I'm your best friend, and you're mine. Now go get cleaned up. Just being around you is making me hungry."

I beat the ten-minute deadline by ninety seconds, and Grace and I were out the door and on our way to Annabeth's studio, with a stop off at Alyssa's place up front first so I could share my condolences firsthand. I wasn't really looking forward to what

was bound to be a hard scene to take, but I needed to do it, if nothing else, for my late friend. I felt in my heart that I owed her that much and more for all that she had given me over the years, and if she had indeed been murdered, I wanted to be the one who found her killer.

CHAPTER 8

AS I DROVE US OVER to Alyssa's house in my Jeep, I said, "I wish I had some donuts to take to the people we're going to be talking to today."

"So you sold out early," Grace replied. "That's a good thing, remember?"

"Of course it is," I replied. "As much as I appreciated all of the sales, the support from the people in April Springs was what really counted with me."

"But the influx in your bank account will be nice, too," Grace added.

"No doubt," I said as we neared Annabeth's childhood home. I remembered when her father had built her a studio of her own in back when we'd started high school, something we had all been jealous of at the time. It was originally intended to be a hangout for Annabeth and the rest of us, a place for young teens to get away and still be close by, but Annabeth had decided from the very start that this would be her private space, restricted solely to her art. I had been one of her best friends, and I'd been inside it only twice in my life. She guarded that part of her world so closely that I felt honored to even be invited in at all.

"I've never seen her studio, at least not on the inside," Grace said. "What's it like?"

"It's been a long time, but on my last visit, it was flooded with northern light, and there were half a dozen easels with works in progress on each of them. Annabeth liked to flit back

and forth between projects back then. She claimed that it gave her perspective to give herself breaks. I expect it's much the same now, despite her recent success."

"She really was getting to be quite popular, wasn't she?" Grace asked me.

"She placed her art all over the world, not to mention the success she had with her corporate logo business. It wouldn't surprise me at all if she made millions."

"Wow, that much? Who gets it all with her death? Is there any way it doesn't all go to her mother?" Grace asked me.

"I have no idea, but the point is we don't know, do we? The question is, how do we find out? I wonder if the will has been filed with the probate court yet."

"We can swing by there after we talk to Alyssa if you'd like," Grace suggested. "Or should we go now?"

"No, I need to see her right away before I lose my nerve." I was dreading the visit, and I wanted to get it over with as soon as possible. I still wasn't sure what I was going to say to this woman who had so recently lost her daughter, but I hoped the words would find me when the time came. It had been my experience in the past that just showing up and offering my sympathies were the things that really mattered. What I said would soon be forgotten, but the important part, the part that showed them I cared, was always significant.

"Okay. I understand. Do you want me to wait in the car while you talk to her?"

I thought about Grace's offer for a few moments before I answered. "Ordinarily I would say no, but I kind of feel this is something I need to do by myself. Do you mind?"

"No, there's plenty for me to do here. I have my phone with me, so I can go online and do a little more digging while you're talking to Alyssa. I want to know about Kerry Minter, and I can't help wondering what Max and Sarah Flowers's names are doing

on that list. You and Alyssa make sense, but Max and Sarah? I don't get those two."

"Well, don't get too wrapped up in your research. I shouldn't be too long," I said.

"Take all of the time you need," Grace said as I pulled up in front of Annabeth's childhood home. I knew that she had a place in town, a neat little condo that she claimed was perfect for her needs, but I had known her when she'd lived here as a girl, and that was where I thought of as her home. It was a quaint little place, barely big enough for the three of them when she and her father had been alive, but I was willing to bet it felt too large to Alyssa now that her husband and her daughter were both gone. What was left for her there now but memories and ghosts? If something happened to Jake, I wasn't sure I could bear continuing to live in the cottage, even though I'd grown up there. The lingering presence of some memories would most likely be too much for me to take, though I hoped I never had the opportunity to find out what I'd do if something happened to my husband. It was a thought I could barely stand contemplating.

Alyssa answered my knock, and I could see instantly that she'd been crying, and very recently at that. "I'm sorry. I can come back later," I said as I started to back out of the doorframe. Grace and I wanted to start our investigation immediately, but at what cost to this poor woman?

"No, it's fine. Come in, Suzanne." Her frame had always been lithe, but now she looked positively gaunt, and I wondered if she'd even been bothering to eat lately or getting more than a few hours of sleep a night.

I did as I was instructed, though, and walked inside. The house felt small to me, but that could have been because I hadn't been in there for many years. Once we'd all grown up, there hadn't been any reason for me to visit Alyssa anymore with

Annabeth gone. The furniture was faded, and there was a distinct air of sadness to the place. Mounted over the piano—an ancient upright—there was a mini shrine to Annabeth's childhood. I felt myself flashing back to when most of the photos had been taken. After all, I'd been such an integral part of her life back then that it astounded and saddened me now how much we'd drifted apart since school. We were still cordial, even friendly, but she and Grace and Trish and I had been so close that I wouldn't have believed we'd ever be apart. That was one of the things time stole from us, though. It took work on everyone's part to stay close, and with all of the distractions of being an adult, sometimes it was easier just to let things, and people, drift silently away. I vowed not to let that happen with Grace and Trish. I suddenly realized that I'd been staring at Annabeth's youthful photos for a very long time. When I looked away from them to Alyssa, I said, "I'm sorry. These bring back a flood of memories for me. I can't believe how close we once were. I should have been a better friend to her."

To my surprise, Alyssa put her arm around my shoulder, trying to offer *me* comfort, even though she had suffered a much greater loss in Annabeth's death than I could imagine. "She loved you so much, Suzanne. You might not realize it, but she didn't have many real friends in the past few years. She always spoke so highly of you."

"You must miss her terribly," I said. "I'm so very sorry for your loss."

"Thank you," she said automatically, no doubt hearing the words of consolation repeated ad infinitum over the past several days. "I suppose you're wondering about my odd behavior at your shop this morning."

"I understand you not wanting to come in," I said.

"The truth is, I owe you an apology," Alyssa said, and then I noticed that tears were creeping down her cheeks.

"Why on earth do you say that?"

"I should have let your mother call you as soon as she found out about Annabeth, but I wasn't in my right mind at the time. You had every right to be at the funeral to say good-bye to her properly, and I failed you both miserably." Her tears were streaming down her cheeks fiercely now, though she made no move to wipe them away.

"No apologies necessary. I understand your reasoning," I said, all of the hurt I'd felt from being excluded washed away by a grieving mother's tears. "Not that there's anything to forgive, but we're good, Alyssa."

She smiled through her tears, and then she hugged me again. "You always were a good girl. Thank you." Stepping away from me, she said, "I'm so glad you came by. Would you like something to eat? I have casseroles and desserts overflowing my kitchen, and I'll *never* eat it all."

"Are you at least eating *some* of it?" I asked her. It may have been a bit presumptuous, but I was sincerely worried about the woman.

"I do my best," she said, "but I just don't seem to have an appetite these days."

I wasn't sure how to bring up the second reason for my visit, but to my surprise, Alyssa did it for me. "Suzanne, since you're here, would it be too much to ask you for a favor?"

"Anything," I said, and I meant it quite literally. I knew Annabeth would do the same if our roles were reversed and it was Momma asking her for a favor, so I didn't even hesitate.

"I haven't been able to bring myself to go into Annabeth's studio since that dreadful day. Would you take a look around and make sure everything is all right in there? I keep having nightmares of sinks running over with water and fires starting in corners, but I just can't bring myself to go in."

"I'm more than happy to help," I told her. "Do you mind if Grace comes in with me?"

"Grace is here?" Alyssa asked as she moved to a window and lifted a curtain aside. "Why didn't she come in with you?"

"I wanted to speak with you alone," I admitted. "I hope that's okay."

"It's fine. By all means, ask her to go with you. I'm sorry, I just can't bring myself to do it."

"Consider it done," I said.

I started to beckon to Grace when Alyssa said, "Hang on one second. You'll be needing the key. Annabeth was very particular about who went inside. You and Grace would be two of the few people she would ever welcome there. You can bring the key back after you're finished."

"We shouldn't be too long," I said as Grace got out of the Jeep and approached.

"Please, take your time. I'll be here. After all, there's nowhere else for me to be now." That last bit was said with such an air of sadness that it nearly broke my heart all over again.

I couldn't think of anything to say in response, so I simply gave her one more brief hug, and then I met Grace outside.

"How did it go?" Grace asked me.

"It was fine," I said.

She looked at me askance. "Really? If that's the case, then why are you crying?"

"Am I?" I asked, wiping at my cheeks and being surprised to find them damp with my tears. It had been a necessary thing for me to do, but it had taken more out of me than I'd realized. Somehow, spending time with Alyssa remembering Annabeth had been more trying for me than I'd ever imagined. The loss of my friend had suddenly become more real than it had since I'd heard the news that she was gone. "Okay, I'm not great this second, but I'll be okay."

Grace put her arm around my shoulder. "I know you will," she said. "Was it okay with her for us to look around the studio?"

"I didn't even have to bring it up. She was the one who suggested it. Alyssa has been worried about it, and she asked me if we'd check things out for her."

"We can certainly do that," Grace said as we took the path around the house that led to Annabeth's studio. It was the coolest structure I'd ever been in, and I'd often envied it over the years. The roof was at an angle, and clerestory windows lined the high part, which must have flooded the place with natural sunlight. It was no more than three hundred square feet, but it even included a small loft and a bathroom to boot. Annabeth had gotten a small refrigerator for Christmas one year, and she'd boasted that all she needed was a stove and a sink and she'd be able to live there year-round. For heat and cooling, she'd told me a few years before that she'd paid to put in a split unit that provided all of the comfort she needed.

"Aren't you coming, Suzanne?" Grace asked me.

I hadn't even realized that I'd stopped as I stood there taking it all in. "Sure. Sorry about that."

Grace touched my shoulder lightly. "Take all of the time you need. I know how close the two of you were."

"You were friends with her, too," I protested.

"Sure, but the two of you were artists, and I never made any claims to be one myself."

"I may have been a budding one in school, but those days are long gone," I admitted a little regretfully.

"Suzanne, you're a young woman, relatively speaking."

"Hey, you're the same age as I am," I protested.

"Like I said, it's all relative. Anyway, it's not too late to take it up again. Even if you don't, you're an artist in making donuts. That should count for something."

"I don't know about that," I said after biting my lower lip for a moment.

"You've *never* given yourself enough credit for the things that you do extraordinarily well. Trust me, you could give me the same ingredients you use every day, and you would produce a masterpiece, while mine wouldn't even be edible."

"Grace, you have your own special skill set," I said in consolation.

"You'd better believe it, baby," she answered me with a grin.

"Did you really just call me 'baby'?" I asked her.

"Yeah, I thought it sounded funny as it came out, too. Anyhow, let's go take a peek, shall we?"

"We shall," I said, suddenly feeling better after my conversation with Grace. She had that effect on me most of the time, and I knew I had chosen my best friend wisely all those years ago.

As I unlocked the front door and stepped inside, I took in the space. As I'd expected, there were four canvasses in different stages of completion spread around the room, but none of them matched the one I'd so recently received from Annabeth. Was that significant? Had she gone through a dark period and then somehow managed to pull herself out of it, or had she simply found a way of disguising it for everyone else? The paintings on display at the moment had subject matters that were eclectic, to say the least. One featured a dazzling waterfall that seemed to glisten with colors, while one was a night scene, resplendent in velvety dark undertones and only a single source of light illuminating the subject matter. The third painting was a portrait in its earliest stages, and the final one was, to my surprise, a large lovely donut, iced and sprinkled and looking good enough to make me want to lick the canvas. There was a surreal quality to it that elevated the mundane donut to an object of lust and desire to all who beheld it.

Then again, maybe that was just *my* reaction to it.

"Will you look at that?" Grace asked as she gravitated toward the last one I'd studied. "This had to be the real painting she promised you!"

"It's amazing," I said. The painting was complete as far as I could tell, though I couldn't see Annabeth's signature anywhere on it, so evidently she wasn't quite satisfied with it yet. I loved it and wondered if there was any way Alyssa would let me buy it from her. I was certainly going to ask, but in the meantime, I looked around the studio. It was organized chaos, with things spread out haphazardly, oil and watercolor paint tubes everywhere, drop cloths on the floor in several places, and shelves full of brushes, palettes, knives, water cups, bottles of turpentine, and books, wow, the books! One wall was taken over completely by shelving that offered books on art from floor to ceiling. Evidently Annabeth loved to study what those who had come before her had done. It was an impressive collection, no doubt worth more than I could even imagine. There was one noticeable hole on the shelves though, and as I looked around, I found the thick volume that probably fit in the empty space. It was titled *Watercolor Techniques*, and as I flipped through it, I was surprised by how basic the text seemed to be. Annabeth was an accomplished artist in many mediums, from oils to pencils to charcoals to watercolors. So why would she need to refresh her basic techniques? There was more here than met the eye. I picked up the book and started leafing through it. As I did, I saw something tucked in between two pages and went back to find it. There was a bank withdrawal slip for ten thousand dollars, and it was dated two days before she'd died. Why had she needed that much money so recently? What had happened to it? Had she spent it, or was it still somewhere in the studio?

"Grace, look at this," I said as I called out to her. "What do you make of it?"

She whistled softly under her breath. "It appears that Annabeth was about to go on a shopping spree."

"Why do you say that?" I asked her.

"If I had that kind of money to pull out of my account on a whim, that's what I'd use it for," she explained.

"I wouldn't," I said.

"Are you judging me, Suzanne?" she asked wryly.

"No, not at all. I'm just saying that she must have had her own reasons. I wonder what she spent it on?"

"Who says she spent it?" Grace said. "She could have needed it for something else."

"Like paying off a blackmailer?" I suggested.

"Wow, what made your mind go straight to that? It could have been perfectly innocent."

"I wish you were right, but I can't think of any other reason at the moment. We need to ask Alyssa about this," I said as I tucked it back into the book and set it aside. "Have you found anything interesting?"

"Just this," she said as she held up a small datebook/calendar.

"What's in it? Is there anything we can use?"

"I looked at the last few entries," Grace said. "She was meeting someone a few days before she died, but I don't know who it was. There aren't initials or anything, just a note that says, 'Be careful.' That sounds a bit ominous, doesn't it?"

"It does," I said. "Where was she meeting them, and at what time?"

"Ten p.m. in back of the library in Union Square," she read off.

"After they were closed for the night. That library isn't in the greatest part of town. Wasn't she afraid to meet someone late at night alone?"

"I don't know, but I know that I would be," Grace readily admitted.

"Me, too. So why go at all?"

"Maybe she was giving them the money she withdrew from her account," Grace said softly.

"Maybe, but if so, why do it in cash? If it was legit, why not just write whoever it was a check?" I asked.

"They probably didn't want a paper trail," Grace said.

"We need to find out who she was meeting," I said. "Is there any chance Alyssa might know?"

"They were close, but I'm not sure they were *that* close," Grace said.

"So, that's one more question we need to find the answer to," I answered. "Let's take it with us, too. I'm already grabbing this book," I said.

"Brushing up on your own skills, Suzanne?" she asked me.

"No, but that's the excuse I'm going to use when I ask Alyssa if I can borrow it."

"We could always just take everything in question and return it all when we're finished with them," Grace suggested.

"No, I can't do that. Alyssa trusted us to do this, and I won't betray her. Hey, what was that?"

"What was what?" Grace asked me.

"I thought I saw someone spying on us from outside that window," I said as I hurried for the door.

By the time I got there, if there had been anyone there in the first place, they were gone now.

"Curiouser and curiouser," Grace said.

"I don't like this," I said. "I don't know about you, but I'm beginning to believe that Annabeth wasn't being paranoid at all when she suspected that someone was after her. I get a creepy vibe from this place, do you?"

"Not really, but you've always been more sensitive to that kind of thing than I am. It's not really surprising though, is it? After all, she did die here."

I looked at the ladder on the floor that must have been up against the wall when she'd fallen—or been pushed. I leaned over and studied it, but if there was anything there, I couldn't see it. I had been hoping for some direct evidence of tampering, like saw marks or loose screws, but it looked as though it was perfectly fine, and I was certain that the police had given it just a cursory look before dismissing it as an accident.

As I stooped over to pick it up and put it back in its place, Grace asked me, "What do you think you are doing?"

"I'm going to climb up and see what Annabeth was reaching for in the loft," I explained.

Grace put a hand on the ladder before I could climb up. "I don't think so."

"It's perfectly safe," I said.

"Tell that to Annabeth," Grace answered as she looked over the ladder for herself after pulling it back to the floor.

After she looked at it for a few moments, I said, "It's fine, just like I said."

"I'm not so sure about that," Grace said as she pointed to the top rung's left side and prodded it for a moment. As she pulled slightly on it, the rung gave way under her pressure, sliding out just enough to loosen it, but not enough to pull it out entirely. "This isn't just where she died, Suzanne. I've got a sneaky suspicion this was the murder weapon someone used on Annabeth."

"Do you honestly think it's loose enough to throw her off the ladder?" I asked as I checked a few more rungs. "Look, these spin a little, too. It's an old ladder. Chances are Annabeth had been climbing this thing for years like this. She probably knew every loose rung on it." I grabbed the ladder and put it upright again. "Here, I'll show you."

"I think you're crazy, but if you fall and kill yourself, you should know that I'll never forgive you."

"You do realize that it won't be an issue for me if it ends up happening that way," I said with a reassuring smile. The rungs were indeed loose, but since I was expecting as much, it didn't throw me off. Still, if Annabeth had been distracted by something else, I supposed that it was possible that it could have caused her fall. As I climbed up to the top of the loft, I looked back down.

She had supposedly hit her head on the edge of the work table, but I couldn't see any way that could happen, based on the few places the ladder actually fit in the space.

"What's wrong?" Grace asked me from below.

"I'm starting to think she wasn't on the ladder at all when she died. I believe someone staged it to *look* like a fall, but what really happened is they must have snuck up behind her and hit her hard enough to kill her. How hard would that have to be?"

"Not hard at all, if they hit her in the right spot," Grace said. "I wonder what they used to do it, but the real question is, who was it that killed our friend?"

"Well, we have a list, so we can start looking for them. Grace, Annabeth wasn't being paranoid. I believe someone was actually trying to kill her, and what's worse, they succeeded."

CHAPTER 9

"**I** wish Stephen was here," I said a minute later as I looked around for something that might have been used as a murder weapon.

"I do, too," Grace replied. "What has that got to do with anything?"

"If he was around, we could take this to him. If Jake was in town, we could ask for his opinion as well, but I don't have a lot of faith in Rick and Darby to find a murderer who is clearly pretty clever."

"We could always ask George," Grace said, "or even Phillip for that matter."

"Yes, I suppose we could, but they don't have any more official standing than we do," I said. "It's not like we need them to investigate this for us."

"That's true enough," Grace said. "Besides, even if Jake and Stephen were out in the Jeep waiting for us, we probably wouldn't consult with them, at least not until we had something solid to pass on to them. Right now, as good as our leads seem, we have a great deal of speculation and not a lot of facts to back them up."

She paused for a few moments until I finally had to ask, "Grace, what's on your mind?"

"Don't take this the wrong way, but Suzanne, are you losing your nerve? If you are, I totally get it, but we've never asked for help before."

I wanted to argue with her, but she was certainly making a valid point. Maybe I was losing it a bit, but I couldn't let that happen, not if we were going to find Annabeth's killer. "The only prudent thing to do is to dig into this ourselves," I said instead of answering her question more directly. During my recuperation, I'd often debated whether I ever wanted to get involved with another murder investigation for the rest of my life, but this was Annabeth, not some stranger I barely knew. Whoever had killed her had also destroyed a very important part of my childhood, and they'd taken a good friend away from me as well. If ever there was a case that screamed out for my involvement, this was it. I might have been a little gun-shy, but I wasn't about to let that stop me from doing what I knew I needed to do.

"Then it's settled," Grace said, clearly satisfied with my answer. "From this moment forward, we treat this as a homicide, but we don't tell anyone, and I mean anyone, about our suspicions. It's the only way we're going to be able to snoop around without anyone knowing what we're really up to. Can you keep this from Jake?"

"If I have to. How about Stephen? Can you do the same?"

"Oh, there's *lots* of things I keep from him," she said with a wicked grin.

"Such as?"

"Suzanne, I can't give away *all* of my secrets, even to you. Now let's keep looking until we're satisfied that there's nothing else here for us to find."

"I'm game if you are," I said. As I started digging, I noticed a pile of brown paper sheets much like what we'd found wrapping my painting. Many of these even had writing on them as well. "It appears that Annabeth didn't just use this paper for notes for me. It was a way she left herself reminders. Here's one that says, 'Dry cleaning! Talking Rabbits. Would Everdine go for that? What's wrong with purple? They want *gray*. How boring!' These

go on and on like that," I added as I kept leafing through the sheets. "Hang on a second," I said as I took out my phone.

"Did you find something worth photographing?" Grace asked excitedly.

"No. Well, maybe. I want to check something against what we found on *my* wrapping." I pulled up the image in question and said, "What do you know? We have a winner."

"Did you find the killer's name written somewhere?" she asked.

"No, but I know what those random numbers we found mean," I said as I showed her the sheet. "It's the phone number for Everdine. Unless I miss my guess, she was designing a logo for them, something with rabbits, maybe. The number, if you run it all together, is 1-554-545-9104. I'll bet you dollars to donuts that's their number."

"There's only one way to find out," Grace said as she took out her cell phone. Once she dialed the number, she held her phone out, so I could hear as well.

"Everdine Corporation," the smooth, dulcet-toned woman said with practiced ease. "How may I direct your call?"

"Where exactly are you located?" Grace asked her.

"We're on the corner of Marrimon and Woodridge," she said. "Twenty thirty-five."

"I mean what city are you located in?" Grace pushed.

The woman paused a moment. "We're in Burberry Ridge just outside of Seattle, Washington. May I help you?" she asked, a little more insistently this time.

"You just did," Grace said, and then she hung up. "That was one confused receptionist," she said with a smile. "At least we can strike those numbers off our list. That's some progress."

"Here's a little more, maybe," I said as I pulled another sheet off the stack and found an old-fashioned cell phone buried in the papers. The phone looked fairly new, but I didn't even

realize they were still making flip phones. Its design looked so antiquated compared to mine that it seemed as though it should have been in a museum. "Was this Annabeth's?" I asked Grace.

She took it from me and studied it for a moment before handing it back to me. "I'm not even sure I could make a call on it."

"It's probably more dependable than mine is," I said, remembering the form and function of my old phone before I got one that was supposedly smart. Supposedly. "Let's see," I said as I opened it up and checked out the screen. "Will you look at that? It's got everything you need. There's an address book and even a log of calls that have been made and received." I was interested in Annabeth's contact information, but what was more pressing was the history of her most recent calls. Perhaps there would be a clue there as to who had killed her. I pulled out my phone to compare some of her numbers with mine and found that she'd dialed Max's phone sometime in the three days before she died.

Now it was my turn to make a call. "Hey, Max," I said when my ex-husband answered on the third ring.

"Suzanne, I heard you were back in town! I didn't want to overwhelm you today, but I'd love to see you soon. How are you doing? Emily and I were just talking about you the other day."

"I'm okay," I said. "Listen, I heard you were talking to Annabeth not long before she died. What's up with that?"

"Suzanne, I wasn't cheating on Emily," he said quickly.

"I never said that you were," I replied. "So be a sport and tell me what was going on between you."

"It's nothing, really. I was out for a drive, and I happened to spot her at the side of the road with a flat tire," Max explained. "It was all perfectly innocent."

"Are you trying to tell me that *you* changed a *tire*?" I asked. It was impossible to keep my incredulity from my voice.

"Me? Are you kidding? No way I'd even know how to *begin* to do that. Annabeth didn't have her phone on her, so I let her use mine. We sat in my car until the tow truck came and did it for her. That's it, end of story. Well, she did call afterwards to thank me again, but that was later. I came back and told Emily all about it immediately. She thought it was rather gallant of me."

"Being gallant would have included changing the tire yourself," I said with a smile. My ex-husband was many things, but being handy was not one of them. "If it was all so innocent, why did you feel the need to tell Emily what happened?"

"You're kidding, right? You know how some folks in April Springs are. I know at least two busybodies spotted us together, so I wanted to make sure that Emily heard the truth from me before the tongues could start wagging. Why do you care, if I may ask?"

"You may not," I said with a chuckle. "Thanks, Max."

"You bet," he said. I knew he wouldn't be offended by my refusal to answer his question. In fact, he probably enjoyed it.

"Max is in the clear," I said. "Do you want to call the next one, or shall I?"

Grace nodded. "I'll take care of it. I already looked up the flower shop's number."

Suddenly that entry made perfect sense. "'Sarah Flowers' isn't a name, it's what she does. Sarah, who happens to own the only flower shop in town," I said. "I missed that completely. I must be getting senile."

"You are, but you still have your uses, so I'm not ready to trade you in for a new best friend and partner yet," Grace said with a smile. "If it's any consolation, I just got it a few minutes ago myself." Grace got Sarah on the line and soon established that Annabeth had sent Max a *manly* bouquet to thank him for his help with her tire. I had no idea what a manly bouquet might entail, but this wasn't the time to ask.

After she hung up, I said, "So, Sarah's in the clear, and I imagine Alyssa and I were just reminders for her to touch base with us. You know how Annabeth used to get when she was working on a project. She'd need to set an alarm to eat lunch or go to bed at night when she was focused on a new piece of work."

"I've never had a problem with either one of those things myself," Grace said with a wry smile. "That explains everyone but Kerry Minter. I haven't had a chance to check her out online, so I'll do that right now." Grace tapped a few buttons on her cell phone and read the entry off to me. "It appears that Kerry owns Artie's, some super-duper artist supply place in Union Square. Hey, I've seen her sign! I know where that is; it's on the outskirts of town," Grace said.

"It's understandable why Annabeth would be friends with her, then," I replied.

"What if they *weren't* friends, though?" Grace asked me.

"She was a bubble, not a square," I reminded her.

"Which is *our* interpretation of what we found, based on nothing more than our own intuition," Grace said.

"Okay, we'll go speak with her. I know we have to have chats with Martin Lancaster, Christopho Langer, Bonnie Small, and whoever this Galen is as well."

"At least we're narrowing down our list of suspects."

"Annabeth's list, you mean," I said.

"At this point, aren't they one and the same?" she asked.

"That's a fair point," I said as I caught another movement outside the studio window. Without changing my tone of voice, I edged toward the door in the hopes of catching whoever was there red-handed.

I threw open the door, and I was surprised to find a stranger standing there, looking as though she'd just got her hand stuck in the cookie jar.

"What do you think you are doing lurking around here?" I asked her, clearly catching her off guard. Maybe I was being a bit aggressive, but she was violating Annabeth's space, and I was very protective of my late friend.

The nondescript woman in her mid-fifties clearly decided to push back. "I'm the one who should be asking the two of you that. Now step aside and let me in."

I wasn't about to move, and neither was Grace. It would have taken more than this heavyset woman to push her way past us. "Who exactly are you?" Grace asked her.

"I'm Bonnie Small," the woman said, as though her declaration should mean something to us. A few hours earlier, I wouldn't have had a clue who she was, but after reading the notes from Annabeth and learning Grace's Internet search, I knew exactly who she was. She snapped, "I have more right to be inside Annabeth's studio than you do."

"How can you say that?" I asked her, honestly startled by the woman's brazen behavior. "You don't even know who we are."

"You aren't important," she said. "That's all I care about. Now step aside. I'm warning you, I won't tell you again." She really had an air of authority about her. It might have worked on most folks, but then again, she wasn't dealing with most people.

"We're important enough," I said as I closed the door behind us, effectively shutting her, and us, out.

"Don't make me do something you'll both regret," the woman said, beginning to bluster. It was clear she wasn't used to being defied.

That was just too bad.

"Please, go on," Grace said with a wicked grin. "Show us what you've got. I'm dying to see it."

Grace's open defiance startled her, and I took a moment to interject while she was still trying to figure out how to deal with

us. "We know you were Annabeth's agent," I said. "There's a simple way to resolve this. Let's all go up to the house and ask Alyssa."

As I suspected, that was not something Bonnie Small wanted to happen. "That woman has no idea of the value of what she's got in there," she said with disgust. "Annabeth has been offered a show posthumously, but I can't make it happen if I can't get inside."

"Who made the offer? Was it the Marcast gallery, by any chance?" I asked.

It was a direct hit, though honestly, it hadn't taken that much of a stretch, given the fact that the owner, Martin Lancaster, was among the names listed on Annabeth's sheet.

"What do you know about that?" she asked us both suspiciously. "Who exactly are you, anyway?"

Now she was interested, given that we were more than just a pair of bystanders in all of this. "We are working on behalf of Annabeth's estate," I said as factually as I could manage it. In a very real way, it was true. I assumed that Alyssa was in charge, and we were doing something for her. That was going to be my story until I was contradicted, anyway.

"That may be so, but *I'm* Annabeth's representative," Bonnie Small said defiantly.

Grace must have seen something in the woman's suddenly wavering gaze. "Perhaps while she was alive, but I doubt your agreement lasted beyond the grave. I'll be examining the contract later, so I'll learn the truth soon enough."

It was clearly another direct hit. We could almost *see* the wheels turning in the agent's mind. Bullying and bluffing hadn't worked on us, much to her chagrin. It was clear that she decided to retreat until she could come up with a different angle to come at us. I decided to give her one more nudge. "Let's all go see Alyssa together, shall we?"

Bonnie Small glanced at her watch, and then she said in a huff, "I don't have time for this nonsense. I'll deal with you all later."

"I'm willing to bet that you *think* you will," Grace said as the agent stormed off.

"That was interesting," I said as I watched the art agent retreat. "She tried to bully the wrong people, didn't she?"

"We might have stopped her for the moment, but I have a hunch she'll be back," Grace answered. "What should we do in the meantime?"

"Let's go have another chat with Alyssa," I said.

"How can I have another if I haven't even had the first one yet?" Grace asked me with a smile.

"Are you channeling Alice at the tea party?" I asked her with a grin.

"Maybe, maybe not," she replied with a Cheshire Cat–like smile of her own.

"Let's just grab a few things before we go," I said as I unlocked the door again. I took the butcher paper notes, the flip phone, the watercolor book, and the planner/datebook.

"We should take the donut painting, too," Grace said as she grabbed the artwork in question.

"That can wait," I said. "I feel guilty asking her about it so soon after losing her daughter, anyway."

"Suzanne, it's obvious Annabeth was painting this for you. What can it hurt asking Alyssa if she's willing to sell it?"

"I don't know," I said hesitantly.

"Fortunately, you don't have to. That's why *I'm* here," Grace said as she grabbed the canvas. "Be sure that door is locked tight behind us. We don't want that Small woman getting in because of us."

I didn't have to be reminded. After all, I double-checked the locks at the donut shop every time I left the building.

If someone wanted to try to break in, that was on them, but at least I was going to do my best to keep them out.

CHAPTER 10

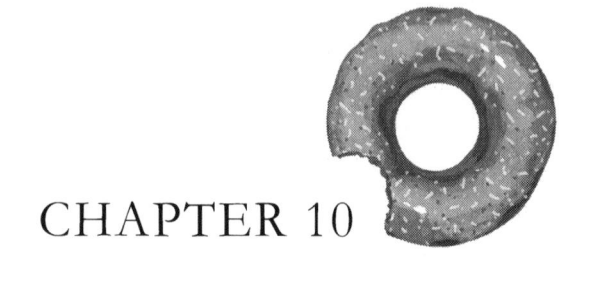

"**A**LYSSA, MAY WE HAVE A few more minutes of your time?" I asked her after she answered the front door.

"Of course. Good, you found it," Alyssa said as she spotted the painting Grace was carrying. "I was about to call you while you were in the studio to tell you about it. In fact, I tried to come out there a few times, but I couldn't bring myself to do it. There are just too many memories there, especially recently."

I knew how much trauma finding the body of someone you cared for could cause, so if anyone could be sympathetic to Alyssa's feelings, it was me. "I totally understand," I said. "I was wondering if I might be able to buy this from you."

"I'm sorry, but it's not for sale," Alyssa said firmly.

I tried to hide my disappointment. "Of course. I understand completely. We'll put it back before we go."

"Suzanne, the reason it's not for sale is because it's already yours. Annabeth painted it to replace the one she gave you earlier. She told me that if anything happened to her, I was to be sure that you got it. It's almost as though she knew she was about to have an accident."

Or be murdered, I thought to myself, though I wasn't ready to share that suspicion with Alyssa just yet. "Are you sure?"

"I'm positive," she said. "Did I see someone out back talking to you a few minutes ago?"

"Bonnie Small was trying to bully her way into Annabeth's

studio, but we wouldn't let her," Grace said bluntly. I couldn't disagree with her assessment of the situation.

"That woman," Alyssa said, nearly spitting the words. "She's the lowest form of leech. Annabeth was getting ready to fire her when she died, but from the way she's been demanding access to my daughter's studio, you would never know they had such a violent argument the day before Annabeth died. The Small woman didn't know I was outside when they were yelling at each other. I was going to bring them some hot chocolate, but I left before either one of them could see me."

"Bonnie didn't give us any indication that they'd had a falling out," I said. It might explain a great deal. In fact, it might even provide a motive for murder, if she had been the one who had killed her client.

"I suppose I'll have to let her in sooner or later, since Annabeth never got a chance to officially fire her," Alyssa said.

"Not necessarily," Grace said. "Do you happen to know where their contract is?"

"I've got it on my desk," Alyssa said. "I've been trying to make sense of it, but I'm afraid I'm not very good at things like that."

"I'm pretty good with them, and I'd be happy to take a look at it for you," Grace offered.

"I would appreciate that so very much," Alyssa said. "I'll be right back," she said as she headed off toward the back of the house.

"You've got a hunch about that agreement, don't you?" I asked Grace.

"I suspect something, but I want to see if I'm right." She didn't have time to explain any further as Alyssa returned with a rather thick document.

Grace took it and flipped immediately toward the back of the agreement. "Let's see...here it is. Termination Conditions.

You're in luck," she said as she glanced at Alyssa. "It says here that upon the death of either the party of the first part or the party of the second, which are Bonnie Small and Annabeth in this case, the document is no longer legally binding and is terminated immediately."

"That explains something I've been wondering about," Alyssa said with a frown. "The day after Annabeth died, that horrid little woman showed up on my doorstep demanding that I sign an addendum to the contract, since I'm Annabeth's executor. She said that it was a formality, but if I didn't do it, I could lose my rights to everything Annabeth had worked so hard to create."

"Do you happen to still have a copy of what she wanted you to sign?" Grace asked. "I'd love the chance to get my hands on it and see exactly what the agent was trying to do."

"I tried to keep it, but she snatched it out of my hand before I could read it all. She was quite upset with me," Alyssa explained.

"I wouldn't worry about it. That seems to be her natural state of being," I said, trying to reassure Annabeth's mother. "Is Annabeth's estate going to be very complicated, or have you had a chance to look into it yet?" I needed to know if anyone besides her mother had anything at stake in Annabeth's demise, and I didn't know how else to ask.

"No, it's as basic as you get. In fact, she'd been after me to make my own will for years, but I'd been reluctant, so she finally talked me into using a computer program. She did hers first to show me how easy it was. Annabeth left everything to me, and I did the same with her. I just never dreamed that she would be the one who died first."

"Did you happen to have the wills witnessed as well?" Grace asked her.

"Yes, we had it done at the bank right after we made them. Did I do the right thing by refusing that nasty little woman's demand?" she asked.

"Absolutely. Alyssa, I know it's none of my business, but would you like some free advice?" Grace asked her.

"Of course I would."

"Don't sign anything, and I mean anything, regarding Annabeth's estate without running it past an attorney first. Your daughter was getting to be rather well known, and as sad as it may seem, her art went up in value the moment she died."

"What a horrible thing to happen," Alyssa said. "Why is that the case?"

"The truth of the matter is that she won't be painting anymore, so what's out there is all there will ever be," Grace said.

I patted Alyssa's shoulder. "Given the circumstances, if you'd like to keep this donut painting, I completely understand."

"No, it was meant for you, Suzanne," she said firmly. "I won't hear another word about it." She looked at the stack of papers and the book in my hands. "What else do you have there?"

I showed her the notes first. "We thought there may be some things that need to be resolved in these," I said. "We promise to bring them back when we're finished with them."

"Alyssa was always jotting things down on that butcher paper," she said softly. Was she going to cry again? Who could blame her if she did, but I wasn't sure I could take it. I had compartmentalized my grief for the moment in order to allow me to focus my attention fully on finding her killer. I'd let my mourning period truly begin only after Grace and I succeeded in our quest.

"Do you mind if we borrow them?" I asked softly. "If you'd rather we didn't, we could photograph them with our phones." I planned on doing that anyway, but I felt as though they might be valuable to have as originals until we were sure there was nothing on them we didn't need.

"No, I realize they are in good hands with you two. Did you happen to find anything else of interest?"

"Just her flip phone, the book on watercolors, and her datebook," I said. "We'd like to hold onto those, too, at least for a bit, if you wouldn't mind."

Alyssa started to nod in agreement when she stopped herself. "Suzanne, what's going on?"

"What do you mean?" I asked her, trying my best to sound as innocent as I possibly could.

"You two are up to something. I've known you both since you were little girls, so don't try to lie to me. What is it?" Before I could answer, she nodded in sudden understanding. "You don't think it was an accident, do you?"

I had two choices: I could lie outright to the woman, or I could tell her the truth.

I'd like to think that it was to my credit that I didn't even hesitate telling her what we suspected. "Alyssa, Grace and I both believe that someone might have had something to do with Annabeth's death."

Grace looked surprised by my admission for a split second, but then she joined in. "We aren't one hundred percent sure of anything yet, but Annabeth had her own suspicions, which she passed on to Suzanne. Alyssa, for our peace of mind, and yours, we want your blessing to dig into this."

Alyssa seemed to collapse on the spot. She barely managed to catch the edge of a chair as she staggered backwards, and for a moment, I thought she was going to tumble right out of it onto the floor. "I'm so sorry! We didn't mean to upset you," I said as I rushed to her aid.

"Suzanne, why do you think I was *really* coming by the donut shop this morning to see you? I believe the same thing. Too many things didn't add up for me after I had time to think about them, and the fact that you are both suspicious as well makes me think that maybe I'm not going crazy after all."

"Alyssa, it's important that you don't share what we're doing

with anyone else," I said. "If everyone believes that Annabeth's death was an accident, we might be able to catch the killer off guard."

"You have my word, but honestly, who would I tell?" she asked. "Annabeth wasn't just my daughter; she was also my best friend. Suzanne, do you think you can find out who did this? I know you and Grace have had some success in the past, but I got the impression the last case you worked on was your final one." Almost apologetically, she added, "Your mother didn't come right out and say it at the funeral, but that was the distinct impression I got."

"I believed it was so at the time, but I'm not about to let someone get away with killing my friend," I reassured her.

"You can count on us. If it can be done, we'll do it," Grace said, doing her best to reassure her of our sincerity and our diligence.

"I have faith in you girls," she said. "What can I do to help?"

"For the moment, besides keeping this to yourself, don't let anyone else into that studio," I said. "In fact, I'd get the locks changed this afternoon."

"No one else had a key," Alyssa said firmly.

"If our theory is right, someone besides Annabeth was there with her the moment she died," I said. "Why take the chance that they had a key?"

Alyssa nodded soberly. "I'll have it taken care of this afternoon. Find whoever did this to my little girl. Promise me."

"We'll do everything in our power to make that happen," I said.

"I have one last favor to ask of you both," Alyssa said as we started for the door.

"Just name it," I answered.

"When this is all said and done, will you two come back and clean out the studio for me? The last thing Annabeth would want would be for me to keep it as it is right now as a shrine in

her honor. I would do it myself, but I think it might break me once and for all if I ever stepped foot inside it again."

"We'll take care of it ourselves," I said, and Grace nodded in agreement, not even trusting herself to speak.

Once we were outside, I looked at Grace for a moment. "If you start crying, I'm not going to have a chance."

"I'm not crying," she said, though it was clear a few tears were tracking down her cheeks. "This is just from the cold."

"Then let's get inside my Jeep and warm up," I said, doing my best not to let my pain escape. Instead, I needed to channel it and track down this killer.

"Where should we start our investigation?" Grace asked.

"I'd like to have a word with Martin Lancaster," I said. "How do you feel about visiting an art gallery?"

"I think it's a smashing idea," she said, and we headed off to Maple Hollow to speak with someone Annabeth clearly suspected might be a candidate for committing her own murder.

"You aren't going to get away with this, Marty," a shapely young woman with short black hair and a dozen piercings in her ears and on her face said as she confronted a heavyset man in his late fifties in front of the art gallery. She wore jet-black slacks and a matching top, and I had to wonder if that was her image of what an artist should look like instead of how she preferred to dress. "We'll see what Bonnie has to say about this!"

"Galen, I'd appreciate it if you'd lower your voice when you address me," the gruff man said. He was clean-shaven, his hair was cut short, and he wore an expensive suit. We'd driven to Maple Hollow to the new Marcast gallery, and Grace and I had been sitting out front in the Jeep trying to come up with

an approach to get us in the door that wouldn't make the art gallery owner suspicious. It had been quite a surprise when the two combatants had burst out of the gallery in full-on conflict. Galen looked as though she wanted to kill him on the spot. When he spoke again, his voice was heavy with sarcasm. "Feel free to speak with Bonnie. After all, that's what agents are for. She agreed to the percentages, so if you have a problem with them, talk to her, not me. You always have another option, you know."

"What's that?"

"Show your work somewhere else, that is if you can find someone willing to do it. I hear the bowling alley in Union Square is looking to add a classier element to their lanes, and there's always the Hideaway Motel on Route 57. Maybe they need new artwork for their rooms."

Galen took a step toward the gallery owner and raised her hand as if to strike him. He stood his ground, and his voice grew hard as he said, "Be very careful, young lady. Your future could depend on your next action."

Galen's fury stalled, and then she seemed to think better of attacking him. "This isn't over," she spat out.

"As far as I'm concerned it is," Martin Lancaster said.

He turned on his heels and went back inside, leaving Galen standing there in front of the gallery still fuming.

"Should we let her cool off before we approach her?" I asked Grace.

My best friend's hand was on the door handle before I could stop her. "Are you kidding? We might be able to get something good out of her if her guard isn't up. Let's go."

I had no choice but to follow Grace and head toward the artist. Maybe she was right. In times of great emotion, most people were less guarded than normal, though I had a hard time seeing this woman as anything but volatile.

As we joined her, Grace asked, "You're Galen, aren't you? I've heard all about your fantastic artwork."

It was a solid approach. After all, it's hard to go wrong telling a new mother that her baby is beautiful. "I have a certain following," she said stiffly as she took us in. "Try telling that to him, though," she said angrily.

"Doesn't he appreciate you?" I asked her.

"He cares only about *money*," Galen said. She made the last word sound as though she were cursing.

"I'm surprised your agent didn't handle him better," Grace said. "Then again, we've met Bonnie Small, so maybe I'm not all that surprised after all."

Galen's glance sharpened. "You're not clients of hers, too, are you?"

"No, I make donuts for a living," I admitted, "and she works for a cosmetics company."

"Then how do you know Bonnie?" Galen asked, clearly still suspicious of us.

"We were friends of Annabeth Kline," I admitted.

Galen shook her head briefly. "I'm sorry she's dead, but the woman was a hack, plain and simple. Do you know she also designed corporate *logos*? Who was she trying to fool claiming to be a real artist?"

I had to literally bite my tongue to keep from firing back at this woman. She was attacking my late friend, and if I hadn't been trying to solve Annabeth's murder, I would have let her have it with both barrels. Fortunately, Grace had a bit more composure than I did. "Does that mean you two didn't get along?"

"We tolerated each other," she admitted. "We had to, since we were both clients of Bonnie's, and the art world around here is a very closed circle." After a few seconds, she amended her earlier statement. "Truth be told, I suppose she wasn't that bad.

It's ridiculous what her pieces are going to be worth now that she's dead, though."

"I wouldn't be too jealous," I said as sweetly as I could muster. "After all, the same thing will happen as soon as you're gone, too."

She seemed to take solace in that fact. "There's always that," Galen said, not taking offense at the inference that she wouldn't be around all that long. "Not that I'll be here to enjoy it." She took us in again. "What are you both doing here?"

"We heard about the gallery and wanted to come by and check it out for ourselves," I said.

"If you're looking to buy some genuinely good art, drop by my studio. I can offer you a *much* better deal than you'll ever get here." She handed us both business cards just as her cell phone rang. After glancing at the number, she said, "Sorry, but I've got to get this." With that, she walked away, screaming at whoever was on the other end of the line almost immediately.

The woman had a temper worse than any I'd ever seen, and I had a hunch that it could be fatal to cross her. Was that what had happened with Annabeth? "She sure acted as though she hated having to stoop so low as to charge money for her artwork," I said.

"True, but she wasn't too good to try to go around her agent and the gallery, though," Grace said as she tapped the card in her hand. "Maybe we can use that to our advantage."

"We don't actually have to *buy* anything of hers, do we?" I asked.

"No. Have you seen her work?"

"Hardly. I just don't want to support that particular artist, if you know what I mean," I said. "I doubt she's to my taste, anyway."

"I saw some of her work online. It's all pretty dark stuff," Grace agreed. "Are you ready to tackle Martin Lancaster?"

"We might as well," I said as I tucked Galen's business card into the pocket of my jeans. "He can't be any worse to deal with than she was."

"I've got a hunch that he's going to be unpleasant to deal with in his own way," Grace said. "The man was so condescending to her, I was kind of surprised Galen restrained herself despite his threat."

"He must have a lot of power over her," I said.

"If she can't exhibit her work, she can't sell anything," Grace said. "Suzanne, how would you like to pose as a freelance artist looking for a show?"

"Grace, I haven't painted anything in years. What do I do when he asks to see my work?"

She just laughed. "You heard him before. Do you honestly think he's going to even ask?"

"I don't know," I said reluctantly.

"Okay, then *I'll* be the artist," Grace crowed. "That sounds more like fun anyway."

"No offense, but you have even less talent than I do," I said.

"None taken," she said with a grin. "I'm betting we won't have to worry about that, though."

I stopped her before she could go in. "I have another idea that might be better. You're dressed too nicely to be a starving artist. Why don't you be a collector instead? I'm willing to bet that he'll be a lot nicer to you if he thinks you're buying instead of selling."

Grace thought it over for a few moments. "You've got a point. Okay, we'll play it your way, though it would have been a great deal more fun my way." She took in my outfit before she asked me, "Who are you supposed to be?"

"How about your best friend, just tagging along?" I asked her.

"That could work," Grace said. "Let's go inside."

CHAPTER 11

MARTIN LANCASTER WAS STANDING AT a desk in the back of the gallery making notes in a large ledger when we walked in. "May I help you?" he asked, gravitating toward Grace, much as I'd expected he would. A stylish young woman, clearly his assistant, was standing nearby. "Cara, three coffees, please."

The assistant looked at him with scorn when she thought he wasn't looking in her direction, but she hadn't taken into account that *we* were watching her. She blushed a bit as she turned to do as he said, but then the gallery phone rang. "What should I do?" she asked him.

"Always get the phone first!" he snapped. This was clearly not a good man to work for, no matter what else he might be. He looked back at Grace, and his stern look melted into a plastered-on smile. "Now, is there anything in particular I can do for you ladies today?"

"I'm looking to acquire a few pieces for my growing collection," she said.

You could almost see the greed in his gaze. "You've come to the right place. Here at Marcast, we specialize in local artists on their way up. Not only will you find great value, but I can assure you that it will appreciate astronomically over time."

It was a bold statement, impossible to guarantee, but he somehow managed to make it with a straight face. "May I ask what your collection looks like now?"

"You may. I've been focusing on Annabeth Kline lately. I just got back from a very successful business trip to Paris, and I find myself wishing to expand my collection. Do you happen to have any of her works on hand?"

"You haven't heard the news, have you?" Lancaster asked. "I'm afraid she's passed away."

"What?" Grace asked, pretending to be shocked by the knowledge. "What happened to her?"

"As I understand it, she had an unfortunate accident in her studio," he said. "We don't currently have any of her works in our inventory, though we are due to get some soon, but we do have pieces by Galen and Christopho Langer on hand. They are both *very* hot properties at the moment."

He hadn't acted that way earlier when we'd heard him fighting with Galen, but that was to be expected. Grace managed to sound disappointed with his offerings, though I had a hunch he could have offered her two Monets and a Degas and she would have sounded exactly the same. "I had my heart set on a new Annabeth Kline."

She turned to go, and I knew better than to try to stop her. When Grace was running the questioning, I'd learned to just sit back and follow her lead.

"As I said, I will be getting her last works very soon," Lancaster said quickly, nearly trying to get around us and cut our escape off.

"Really? How so?"

"I'm finalizing negotiations with her representation, and I've been assured that everything she has completed will be here within a matter of days. If I could get your number, I'd be happy to call and let you know when they arrive, though they will probably be quite a bit more expensive than your earlier pieces."

"I understand that," Grace said gruffly.

"Your number?" he asked again. His assistant approached

with the three promised coffees, but he waved her away. I wasn't sure we were going to get out of there without giving him something; the man was really persistent.

"How was your relationship with the artist?" I asked him, ignoring his request.

He glanced at me as though I was merely an obstacle in the way of him making a big fat sale, but Grace nodded as she added, "Did you know her very well?"

"Quite well, as a matter of fact," Lancaster said. After lowering his voice, though his assistant was well out of earshot, he added, "I was her confidante for the last several months. We were *very* close."

"Are you implying a *physical* relationship?" Grace asked him with a grimace.

"I don't feel right discussing that with you." The full-on implication was that they had been together in a more intimate setting than the art gallery, but since I couldn't refute it, I decided to let it slide. "I'm truly sorry about that. She came to me for some advice, and I was able, in my own small way, to help her. In fact, it wouldn't be overstating things to say that we were about to embark on a show in the very near future that would have put her over the top."

"Don't those things normally go through agents?" Grace asked.

"Bonnie Small was on her way out," Lancaster said. So, that confirmed what Alyssa had told us earlier. What was Lancaster's angle? If he were going to be taking over for Bonnie, he would have made more money with Annabeth alive, not dead. That depended on if he was telling the truth though, which was a very big *if*. "Now, about that number. I'm afraid I really must insist."

He could insist all he wanted to, but that didn't mean that he was going to get what he wanted. I had a hunch we'd gotten all we were going to get out of him at the moment, and Grace

must have come to the same conclusion. "I'll check with you tomorrow. Let's hope you have better news for me then."

"I'm sure I will," he said reluctantly as we left.

"That guy is as oily as they come, isn't he?" Grace asked me as we got into the Jeep and drove away. "After talking to him, I feel as though I need a shower."

"I don't know. I thought he was pretty well groomed, for a snake," I said. "Wow, I can't imagine Annabeth having to put up with people like him and Galen and Bonnie Small."

"The art world can be quite a morass," Grace said. "Galen was clearly jealous of Annabeth's success. Bonnie could have been furious that she was leaving her, but what motive could Lancaster have for wanting her dead?"

"What if it wasn't business related? He implied that they were close on a personal basis," I said. "In fact, I'm going to call Alyssa right now and see what she knows about both of them."

"Put it on speaker," Grace said. "I want to hear, too."

"You bet," I said. After Alyssa came on the line, I told her, "We just spoke with an artist named Galen and a gallery owner named Martin Lancaster. Do you know anything about either one of them?"

Alyssa's voice immediately took on an icy edge. "My daughter told me that Galen confronted her about being a hack the day before she died, and Lancaster made a very blunt pass at Annabeth a little later, one which she angrily refused."

"What was Galen's problem with her?" I asked her.

"Her success, most likely. She claimed that Annabeth was a phony, and she was going to expose her to the world as a fraud."

"If *anyone* was a true artist, it was your daughter," I assured her.

Alyssa laughed bitterly. "Thank you, but I know that myself. Galen's work is dreadful, and Annabeth said when she pointed that out to her, clearly tired of the woman's constant attacks,

Galen told her that she'd pay for the insult." Alyssa paused for a few moments before adding, "I probably should have mentioned that before. It's just so hard for me to accept the fact that someone did this to my daughter, that it was no accident."

"We haven't been able to prove anything yet, but we're working on it," I reminded her. "What about Martin Lancaster?"

"He made it sound as though she wouldn't be able to show any of her works in his gallery unless she was a little more receptive to his advances," Alyssa said. "It wasn't the first time he'd made a pass at her, but evidently they had become much more aggressive lately. It was the last thing Annabeth told me, in fact. I should have done something about it then."

"What could you have possibly done, Alyssa?" Grace asked gently. "Who knew this was going to happen?"

"Do you think one of them hurt my little girl?" Alyssa asked, the anger thick in her voice.

"That's what we're trying to find out. Is there anything else you know that you haven't told us about her group of acquaintances? We're going to go speak with Christopho Langer and Kerry Minter in Union Square next."

"As far as I know, Chris and Annabeth were friends. They had some kind of a misunderstanding a few nights before she died, but I don't know what it was about. The truth is that it wasn't all that unusual for them to have spats, but I know they were close," Alyssa said. "Kerry owns Artie's, so they've known each other for years."

"How did the two of them get along?" I asked.

"Fine, I suppose. I feel like such a fool for not telling you about Galen and Lancaster earlier."

"Don't beat yourself up about it. You've got enough on your mind right now," I said. "We'll talk more later. Bye for now." Grace reached over and ended the call on our end.

"I don't blame Alyssa for not telling us about Galen and

Lancaster," Grace said as I drove toward Union Square. "Why should she want to think about *anyone* who might have killed her daughter?"

"Right now that's our job," I said. "At least we might find a few allies of Annabeth's when we talk to our next two witnesses."

"Christopho's name was in a square too though, remember? Maybe their last quarrel was more serious than most of their disagreements in the past. And just because Kerry Minter's name was in a bubble doesn't necessarily mean that she's innocent," Grace answered.

"I know. We have to keep our eyes wide open. Things aren't always as they seem, are they?" I asked.

"No, but we'll figure it out. I have faith in us," she said.

"One way or another, we'll get to the bottom of this."

"I wonder if there might be anything else Alyssa has forgotten to tell us?" Grace asked me a little later on our drive.

"It's possible," I admitted. "We'll just have to dig out the facts ourselves. If we need to confirm anything with her, we've got her as a source, but really, how is this situation different from most of the cases we investigate? It's not all that unusual for us to be out on a limb alone."

"Together though, right?" Grace asked me with a weary grin.

"Always together," I agreed.

"Have you ever been here before?" Grace asked me as we pulled into the parking lot of the art supply store. ARTIE'S was emblazoned across a sign that used to announce the big box store that had inhabited the space before it. It was a sign of the times, these cavernous buildings deserted along our landscapes. April Springs hadn't been large enough to attract any of the large chains during their heyday, and while a few folks had been unhappy about having to drive so far to shop in one, I for one

was happy that small businesses still had a foothold, no matter how precarious, in our towns and hamlets. Sure, the chains might be able to sell their donuts at a cut-rate price, but there was a sameness to them even across the flavors that were okay, not great, but good enough for a great many people. Emma and I strove to present the best product we could to our customers, offering the very highest quality of ingredients we could. I could certainly tell the difference between my fare and those that had been mass produced, but maybe I was just prejudiced. There might come a day when the conveyor-belt donut shops matched my quality, but I doubted it. If and when that did happen, I'd still have something to offer my customers that the chains couldn't touch: personal service. Maybe I was seeing the world through myopic donut glasses, but I felt that way all the way down to my very core, and I wasn't about to give that up.

"Suzanne, where's your mind right now?" Grace asked me, bringing me suddenly out of my reverie.

"I was just thinking about donuts," I admitted.

My best friend laughed. "Boy, you certainly are a gal with a one-track mind, aren't you?"

"Guilty as charged," I said with a grin. "Let's go see Kerry Minter."

"I hope she's more pleasant than the earlier folks we spoke with on Annabeth's list," Grace said.

"They could hardly be any worse, could they?"

"I'm guessing we're playing this straight up, right?" Grace asked.

"I don't know. I was thinking about buying some basic art supplies while we're there," I admitted.

"Just to get her to talk to us?"

"That's part of it, but being around Annabeth's artwork again has inspired me. Maybe it's not too late for me after all."

"You know about Grandma Moses, don't you?" Grace asked

me with a grin. "If she wasn't too old to start painting, you shouldn't be."

"Thanks so much for comparing me to a grandmother," I said dryly.

"You know what I mean," Grace replied. "I think it's wonderful. In fact, I'll buy your first painting, sight unseen."

It was my turn to laugh. "I doubt it will be worth purchasing," I admitted. "It's been quite a few years since I picked up a paintbrush."

"In this, as in all things, I have faith in you."

"I'm glad at least one of us does," I said as I took a deep breath and opened my car door. "Here goes nothing."

The parking lot had held several vehicles, but I wasn't sure if they were abandoned or if folks were parking there and shopping other places, because the massive store was nearly deserted when we walked in. A neat woman in her forties wearing a bright-red smock approached us the second we were inside the door. I didn't even have time to take in the aisles and aisles of materials, offering every medium I knew and a few I didn't recognize. She even stocked supplies for crafts as well. There were sections for card making, soap making, candle making, and more, and I wondered if she'd needed to expand her selection to keep her shop afloat.

"Good afternoon, ladies," she said with a practiced smile. "Was there something I could help you with today?"

"I'm looking to get back into painting," I said.

"Marvelous," she said as though I had just declared that I was going to give her a million dollars. "What medium would you like to tackle first, or would you like basic supplies for oil, watercolor, chalk, pencil, and more?"

"Let's just start with some beginner's watercolor supplies," I said. "My budget is a little limited at the moment."

"You're in luck. We're having a sale," she said, as though the sheer coincidence of my visit was the luckiest thing I could have done today. As she led us to the watercolor section, she asked, "If the question isn't too nosy, may I ask what made you decide to start painting again?"

"An artist friend of mine just died, and I realized just how much I missed it. Did you know Annabeth Kline?" I asked her, watching her expression carefully.

At the mention of Annabeth's name, the woman took a small step backward, accidently knocking down a display of prestretched canvases and easels. "How clumsy of me," she said as she started to collect the fallen items.

Grace and I joined in. "Sorry, I didn't mean to startle you," I said.

"You didn't. I just wasn't expecting the connection between you. It was such a shame what happened to Annabeth," she said, turning her back to us to collect a few easels that had managed to clatter away from the main pile.

"Did you know her, too?" I asked.

"A bit," Kerry Minter said absently.

"Really? I thought you'd know her better than that," Grace pushed as we all stood.

"I suppose I did, as much as anyone really *knew* Annabeth," the art supply dealer said. "The truth of the matter is that I knew her better than most folks did who are claiming otherwise. You said you were friends with her?"

"Grace and I went to school with Annabeth," I admitted. "We knew her most of her life."

"Then there's no harm in admitting to you that we were more than just acquaintances. She and I had coffee once a month before I opened the store, as long as we didn't have anything else

pressing going on. I was more than a little bit envious of her talent, truth be told. That would put me in the majority around here, though. Some of her contemporaries were more than a little smitten with the green-eyed monster."

"Can you think of anyone in particular?" I asked. It seemed like an innocuous enough question, given the way she'd led our conversation in that direction.

"I hate to talk out of turn," Kerry said. "After all, some of them are good customers of mine, and others have a direct interest in the local art world. I don't know if you realize it, but in many ways it's just like junior high school. There are the cool kids, the smart kids, the goof-offs, and all of the rest."

"Which group did Annabeth fit into?" Grace asked. It was an excellent question, one I wished that I'd thought to ask myself. Well, that was why there were two of us.

"She was the rare bird who could flit from group to group without any problem," Kerry said. "In a way, it made her that much more of a target among her peers."

It was clear the art supply owner wanted to say more, but discretion, and the potential loss of business, kept her from saying anything else. I decided it was time to share a little of our experiences. Maybe it would get her to loosen her own tongue. "We've spoken with Galen already. We ran into her at the Marcast gallery. She wasn't a fan of Annabeth's, and neither was Martin Lancaster, from the way he acted. You could almost see the man's eyes light up when he talked about the increased value of Annabeth's art, but that seemed to be the only thing he was passionate about."

"That man has a cash register for a soul," she said grimly, "and as for Galen, Annabeth had more talent in her little finger than Galen does in her entire body. What's worse, she knew it better than anyone. If Galen just spent as much time on her art

as she has on trying to tear her contemporaries down, she might just manage to make something of herself."

"Bonnie Small must have thought a lot of her ability," I said. "We ran into her at Annabeth's studio, and Bonnie seemed to be her biggest fan."

Kerry shook her head. "Bonnie managed to dupe a handful of people into signing with her, promising riches and renown, but she failed to deliver on any of them in a rather spectacular fashion." Lowering her voice for a moment, she added, "Annabeth was leading a revolt of her clients. She was leaving, and she had just about convinced Christopho Langer to leave as well. Everyone knows that whatever Christopho does, Galen soon copies. She's had a crush on him forever, but he's only ever had eyes for Annabeth." She almost said that last bit wistfully, and I had to wonder if Galen was the only woman who had a crush on Christopho.

"Were they dating?" I asked, wondering why I'd never heard about it if it were true. I'd thought Annabeth and I were still close, but it was clear by what I'd learned today that it wasn't all that true anymore.

"No, not that Christopho didn't keep trying. She kept turning him down, though. I don't know why he didn't choose to go after a woman a bit more accessible to him. Annabeth told me the last time we got together that he was getting to be a bit of a nuisance, and she was going to have to say something to him. I didn't envy her that. I'm fairly certain that Christopho isn't used to getting turned down, especially repeatedly by the same woman."

There was something in the way she said his name that set off alarm bells in my head. I decided not to question my gut and pursue it. "Did *you* two ever date?"

Kerry actually blushed a little as she answered, "We went out

a few times in high school, but after that, we decided that we'd be better off as friends."

Based on her reaction, I had to wonder if it had been *her* decision to change their relationship or *his*. I was willing to bet everything in my bank account, even now that it was brimming over with money from Emma and Sharon's generosity, that it had been Christopho's idea. Could Kerry have been jealous of more than Annabeth's talent? Or was it possible that Christopho had grown tired of Annabeth's rejections, and he'd lashed out at her, literally? The deeper we dug into this mess, the more convoluted it became.

Kerry Minter seemed to realize that she'd told us much more than she'd originally intended, because a mask seemed to fall over her face as she pointed to a nearby aisle. "Everything you need is right here. Now, let's get you started."

As I started to pick up a basic set of brushes, paints, paper, and more, Grace and I kept trying to engage Kerry about Annabeth and her other clientele, but she continued to shut us down. I was about to give up when the front door opened, something we all knew instantly because of the bell in back. I hadn't heard it when we'd first walked in, and I had to wonder if Kerry had installed it back there to tell her she had visitors when she was working in the back or maybe even the storeroom.

"If you'll excuse me," she said the moment she spotted her visitor.

"Wow, did you see her light up just now?" Grace asked me softly. "I'm willing to bet that is the great Christopho himself."

"No bet," I said. "Let's go introduce ourselves."

"Are you really going to buy all of that?" Grace asked me as she surveyed my supplies.

"I know it's a lot, but I can swing it."

"Why don't you let me do it? I wasn't able to get you anything

for Christmas, since you weren't here, so I'd love it if you'd let me do it."

"That would hardly be fair, since I didn't get you anything, either," I reminded her.

"You came home," Grace said. "That's the only present I wanted. Besides, if I buy these supplies for you, you'll feel obligated to use them."

"True enough," I said. "Still, I can't ask you to do this."

"Suzanne, you're not asking. Tell you what. Either let me pick this tab up, or I'll come back later and buy you a gift card for more than you'll spend today. It's your call."

I had to laugh, since I knew it was an argument that I wasn't going to win. "On one condition," I said.

"That I get that first painting?" she asked eagerly.

"Goodness no, I'll probably burn it the second I finish it. No, I get to buy you something for Christmas, too."

Grace frowned for a moment, and I could hear that Kerry and Christopho were both raising their voices. "Think about it," I said as I hurried up front. I wanted to get close enough to eavesdrop but not so close that they knew we were listening. It was a fine line we were dancing, but we'd done it before, albeit with varying degrees of success.

"I don't see why you won't have lunch with me, Chris," Kerry said plaintively. "It's not like it's a date or anything. It's just two old friends catching up, commiserating about the loss of a mutual friend."

"She was more than that to me, and you know it," Christopho said. I was getting tired of referring to this man by such a pretentious name. I'd try to call him "Christopho" to his face, but in my mind, he was going to be "Chris" from here on out.

"I know that, but you have to move on with your life. It's not like you were ever going to get anywhere with her, anyway." The last bit had been a blow to the artist, and she realized her

mistake as soon as she'd made it. "I'm sorry. I shouldn't have said that. It wasn't what I meant."

"I'm finished here," Chris said.

He turned to leave, and Grace and I quickly followed him out of the store.

At least that's where we were heading until Kerry put a hand on my shoulder and stopped me dead in my tracks.

CHAPTER 12

"WHERE EXACTLY DO YOU THINK you're going?" she asked me icily.

"I'll be right back," I said, trying to break free. For an art supplies dealer, the woman had the grip of an arm wrestler.

"Not with my supplies you're not," she said.

I'd honestly forgotten I was still holding them. I thrust everything into her hands and then I headed for the door. "We'll come right back."

"This will all be waiting for you at the counter when you do," she said firmly.

I couldn't really blame her. She was just trying to protect her inventory, but Grace and I had an angry artist to catch up with before he managed to get away.

"Excuse me, are you Christopho?" I asked as Grace and I rushed over to his vehicle, an old beat-up station wagon that was at least fifty years old. I was amazed that it even still ran, based on the rough condition of its exterior. If the flakes of rust hadn't been holding it together, I wasn't sure it would be able to make it out of the parking lot.

"No autographs, ladies. I'm sorry, but there's somewhere I need to be."

The man certainly had a massive ego if that's the first thing

he assumed when we called him by name. He was good looking, tall and fit, but he wasn't exactly a movie star. "We were friends with Annabeth Kline," I said simply.

That stopped him in his tracks. "Do I know you two?"

"I sincerely doubt it. I'm Suzanne, and this is Grace," I said.

"As a matter of fact, I've heard of you both," he said.

"Seriously?" I asked. Sure, I was famous in some circles for my donut-making skills, and Grace was a legend within her company, but there was no reason on earth this man should have ever heard of either one of us. And then I got it. "Annabeth mentioned us to you, didn't she?"

"A few times," he admitted. "I'm sorry for your loss," he said sympathetically.

"And we're sorry for yours," I echoed.

"Did Annabeth ever talk to you about me?" he asked, as eager as a new puppy wanting to please its new family.

"She mentioned you once or twice," Grace said. I looked askance at my friend. I knew that Annabeth had never mentioned the man's name to *me* before, but then I realized that she might have loosely been referring to the notes our late friend had left us. I supposed that counted as a mention in a way.

"What did she have to say?" he asked sincerely.

"Only that you were a person standing alone in the field," she replied. While it was true that Chris's box had been a bit away from the others, I thought she was really stretching the truth saying that, but I wasn't about to correct her.

"She was a fine artist, a good woman, and a dear friend," he said.

"I understand you were interested in more than friendship with her," I answered.

"Why? What did she tell you?" the artist asked, his gaze narrowing a bit as he asked.

"Just that you were interested in pursuing more," Grace added. "That's what Kerry confirmed as well earlier."

"Kerry Minter talks too much," Chris said. "It's going to get her into trouble one of these days, and everyone knows it. With all of the online art supply shops there are today, she's a dying breed."

"But you aren't denying the facts, are you?" Grace probed a little harder.

"So I had a crush on her. Big deal. She said she wasn't interested in pursuing it, so I finally got the hint and dropped it. We were friends, above and beyond anything else." He paused a moment before adding, "Did I think she might change her mind someday? Sure, where there's life, there's hope. We squabbled about it a bit from time to time, but in the end, we were friends, and that was what really mattered to both of us. Whether anything could have *ever* happened between us is something we'll never find out now. I'd like to take that ladder she slipped on and break it into a thousand pieces."

"When was the last time you saw her?" I asked. "Was it in her studio?"

The artist looked askance at me, and perhaps I'd pushed a little too hard with my questions, but blast it all, we had to ask if we expected answers. "Annabeth was *very* protective about her workspace," he said.

"That doesn't exactly answer either one of our questions," Grace reminded him firmly.

"Have a good evening, ladies," he said, and then he got into his decrepit station wagon and, to my surprise, actually managed to drive away.

"We seem to make friends wherever we go, don't we?" Grace asked me with a grin after he was gone.

"I didn't know that was what we were trying to do," I said

as I glanced back at the door of Artie's. "Hey, when did that happen?"

"What's that?" Grace asked as she pivoted to look at the door as well. Instead of saying Open as it had before, it now announced that they were Closed. "How are we going to get your watercolor starter kit now?" Grace inquired.

"I suppose we'll have to come back another time," I replied. "I wouldn't mind taking another shot at Kerry Minter after we've gathered a bit more information on her, anyway."

"Does that mean that we're unofficially moving her from a bubble to a square?" Grace asked me.

"I think we have to. I'm not sure what it is, but I have a hunch there's something Kerry isn't telling us, and besides, we still need to ask her about the boxes Annabeth mentioned in her diamonds. We never had the chance when we were inside."

"Not only that, but we forgot to ask Martin Lancaster about the car she mentioned at Marcast. Wow, we're not having a banner day of investigating, are we?"

"We're a bit rusty," I admitted, "but we'll get better at this. We have to. There's no way we can let Annabeth's killer go free."

"In the meantime, what do you think about going to Napoli's for an early dinner? I don't know about you, but I hate to pass up the opportunity to eat there when it's just a few blocks away."

"You twisted my arm," I said. "A great meal would be nice, and besides, it will give us some time to think about what we've learned so far."

"Then it's a date," she said as we got into the Jeep and headed to our favorite Italian restaurant in the world. Though I'd just seen the entire DeAngelis crew that morning, I had no problems running into them again, especially if it meant I was going to get one of their meals.

It wasn't meant to be, though.

At least not immediately.

Grace and I had been seated by Maria, one of Angelica's lovely daughters, for less than two minutes when Kerry Minter herself walked into the restaurant. The moment she spotted us, she walked directly to our table and glared at us.

"Are you two following me?" she asked worriedly.

"How could we possibly do that, when we were here first?" Grace asked her with just as much punch in her reply. My best friend wasn't one who tolerated being pushed around by anyone, and it was one of the traits I admired about her.

Her legitimate question didn't even faze the art supply store owner. "I don't know how you did it, but clearly you somehow managed it. Did you look at my datebook while you were in my shop?"

"How could we possibly do that? Besides, if we wanted to talk to you longer, we would have stayed in your shop before you closed it so suddenly," I explained. "But since you're here, I have something else I want to ask you."

She sighed before she answered, clearly already tired of us. "I'm really sorry about Annabeth, but the truth is that I'm not really interested in answering any more of your questions. I've already said way too much as it is. My friend is dead too, and I want to mourn her in peace, if it's all the same to you," she said as she waved Maria off. "You know something? All of a sudden I think I'd rather eat at home alone."

Kerry started to walk out, so I got up, with Grace close on my heels. I wasn't about to let her off the hook just because she was being a little too sensitive about our line of questioning.

"Are you leaving, too?" Maria asked, clearly concerned by our exit.

"Yes, but no worries, we'll be right back," I said as we headed back out of the restaurant. "Save our table."

"Of course," she said.

We caught up with Kerry in the parking lot before she could go far. "What happened to Annabeth in your shop recently?" I asked her point-blank.

That certainly got her attention. Kerry stopped and turned back toward us. "What are you talking about?"

"We told you that we were Annabeth's friends," I said. "Why *wouldn't* she tell us what happened at Artie's?"

"If she told you about anything, then you shouldn't have to ask me," Kerry Minter said. Actually, she had a point, but we couldn't let that stop us.

While I was fumbling for a response, Grace asked, "Are you really going to make us say it? Annabeth mentioned there were boxes involved in the incident at your shop." It wasn't exactly a lie, at least not in the strictest sense of the word.

"Some boxes fell near her while she was shopping in the store," Kerry explained. "She probably nudged them herself without realizing it. I'm the first to acknowledge that I put too many things in the aisles. Shoot, I tripped over a display myself when you were there earlier, so you saw that for yourselves. She wasn't hurt, so we both figured no harm, no foul."

"What was in the boxes?" I asked.

"Does that really matter? Like I told you, none of them hit her," Kerry replied.

"Well, if they were full of feathers, they wouldn't have done much damage," I explained, "but if you were storing anvils in them, then it would be a different story altogether."

"They were pretty heavy," Kerry acknowledged. "But like I said, she wasn't hurt. I apologized, and that was that, at least as far as she was concerned."

"Where were you when it happened?" Grace asked her, a very good question indeed.

"I was up front helping a new customer. She was looking for something for her granddaughter's birthday, but she left without buying a thing," she said. "If that's why you're asking, I couldn't have knocked those boxes over myself by accident."

"Was anyone else in the store when it happened?" I asked.

Grace nodded and gave me a strong smile. I was just glad that I had some questions of my own to ask.

"I'm sure there were at least a few people there," Kerry answered.

"What I want to know is if any of the following people were shopping there when the boxes fell," I said. "Martin Lancaster. Galen. Christopho Langer. Bonnie Small. Were *any* of them there?"

Kerry looked troubled by my list, but it was clear she wasn't all that thrilled about cooperating. "Give me a break, you two. I don't see *how* I can tell you that."

"So then you have something to hide," Grace said in an accusatory tone.

"I just told you, I wasn't around her when it happened!" Kerry's face had reddened when she'd responded to Grace's accusation, but she quickly managed to get herself under control again.

"But at least *one* of the names on our list was present, or you wouldn't be reacting the way you are," I said as sympathetically as I could muster, stating it as a fact and not a supposition, which up until a few seconds ago, it clearly was.

"Okay, I'll tell you, but you've got to promise me that you won't tell *anyone* who told you." She turned to me and made her appeal. "Suzanne, you know how tough it can be to run a small business. Give me a break here, will you?"

"We won't tell anyone else if there is *any* possible way to avoid it," I said.

"I guess I have to take your word for it. Galen and Christopho were in the store when it happened, too," she finally admitted.

"Could either one of them have done it?" I asked.

"I honestly have no idea. Galen is a wild card, and if Christopho did it, I can't imagine why, but if you're looking for their motivations, you'll have to speak with them about it. I'm going home now, but I want you both to remember your promise. Please don't tell anyone I told you. It could really hurt Artie's, and I'm hanging on by a thread as it is."

"We won't talk," I said, and Grace nodded in agreement.

"Are things really that bad at Artie's?" I asked her, feeling an outpouring of sympathy for a fellow small business owner.

"Well, they aren't great," she said. "I just love art so much, you know? If my business fails, I don't know what I'm going to do with the rest of my life."

I patted her shoulder. "Hang in there. Maybe things will turn around for you soon."

"I surely hope so," she said, and as we left, I felt myself feeling a great deal of compassion for the woman. There had been times in my past that I hadn't been sure I could keep the donut shop open another day, but somehow things had worked themselves out. Not everyone was as lucky as I'd been, though. It was a cold hard world out there and getting tougher for the little guy every day.

As Kerry Minter meekly walked away, clearly a woman beaten down by her circumstances, Grace started after her.

"Where are you going?" I asked her as I put a hand on her shoulder in order to restrain her.

"I'm not finished talking to her yet, are you?" she asked me.

"Grace, maybe this time we just let it go," I told her in as soothing a voice as I could muster. "After all, we got what we

were looking for. She just said that she wasn't close enough to push those boxes over onto Annabeth."

"*If* she's telling us the truth," Grace said. "I still want the name of that customer, so I can confirm what she just told us."

I looked at Grace for a moment before I answered. "Do you honestly think she's going to give us that information willingly? I doubt she even knows who it was herself, but even if she does, she's not going to tell *us*. She's just trying to protect what's left of her business, Grace. What we need to do is ask Galen and Christopho if *they* were at Artie's when it happened. Maybe we can catch someone in a lie that way."

"Maybe," Grace said reluctantly. "You're right. It's the best we can do with what we've got at the moment."

"Hey, cheer up a little. At least we've made *some* progress," I said. "What do you say we get a bite to eat now?"

"Yes, I like that idea," she said, though she still glanced over her shoulder toward Kerry Minter's fleeting back as we walked back into Napoli's.

Angelica was waiting for us at the door. "Ladies, what are you two up to?" she asked us. "Maria said you had words with Kerry Minter in my restaurant."

"I'm sorry," I quickly apologized. I knew that Angelica had been known to banish customers who caused a fuss at Napoli's, and I couldn't bear the thought of not being able to eat there whenever the mood struck me. It would be a tragic loss, and I wasn't being overdramatic describing it that way. "We went outside before anyone raised their voices."

"Tell me all about it," Angelica said as she led us back to our table and pulled out a chair for herself. Once we were all seated, our restaurateur asked, "Suzanne, are you all right?"

"I'm fine, a-okay," I said, a little confused by the question. "Why do you ask?"

"You seem a little stressed, that's all," she said, and then she turned to Grace. "You see it too, don't you?"

"I'd really rather not answer that, if it's all the same to you," Grace said, avoiding making eye contact with either one of us.

"Hang on a second," I said, fighting to keep my voice even and level. "What's going on here? Is this some kind of intervention?"

"Suzanne, you *have* been a little on edge since you got back home," Grace said apologetically. "It's perfectly understandable, but I can't, or I should say I won't, lie to Angelica about it. Admit it. You feel it, too. It's okay not to always be the strongest person in the room, you know." She looked as though she wanted to cry because of her admission.

"We *both* know why I'm stressed right *now*," I said softly.

"I know," Grace said. "I'm sorry I said anything."

"You didn't, at least not willingly, but I did," Angelica said as she reached out both hands and patted ours gently. "Let's go, ladies."

"You're throwing us out?" I asked, my voice full of angst at the prospect of being evicted.

"Of course not," she said with a smile. "You'll be dining in the kitchen where we can chat while you eat," she said as she looked around the room. Angelica had a point. Several of her customers were watching us intently, and no doubt listening in as well, though everyone's attention turned quickly elsewhere when Angelica made eye contact with each and every one of them.

"I'm good with that," I said.

As we followed Angelica into the kitchen, Grace reached over and squeezed my hand. "I'm sorry I said anything just then. Forgive me?"

"Yes, but if you're worried about me, don't wait to tell me in front of one of our friends."

"How about our enemies?" she asked, daring a slight grin.

I had to laugh, she looked so unsure of herself, a rare state of mind for Grace. "In front of *anyone*."

"Agreed," she said.

Once we were in the kitchen, we found Sophia eating one of the donuts they'd bought earlier that morning. "These are so great," she said with a grin, showing raspberry filling on her teeth, powdered sugar on her lips, and a big smile through it all.

"How many of those have you had today, young lady?" Angelica asked her youngest daughter critically.

"Hey, I'm a growing girl," Sophia protested. "I need it."

"Growing, yes, but let's not get carried away," Angelica said, softening her expression.

"I'm trying to restrain myself, but they are just so darn good," Sophia replied, and both women smiled softly at each other. It was clear that Angelica loved all of her daughters equally, but just as clear that her baby had a special place in her heart.

"What happened to putting them on the dessert menu?" I asked with a grin.

"Mom wanted to, but we overruled her," Sophia said with more than a hint of laughter in her voice.

After we were seated at the small family table in the kitchen where we dined at times, Angelica plated up food rather randomly, or so it seemed to me, before placing a dish in front of each of us. I wasn't about to complain. There was nothing on the menu I didn't relish eating, and I knew for a fact that Grace felt the same way. "What is your issue with Kerry Minter?" she asked as we each took our first bites of food.

The amazing textures and tastes weren't lost on me, but the question did dim my enjoyment a bit. "Angelica, we can tell you, but it can't leave this kitchen."

"Ooh, speak up a little. I want to hear, too," Sophia said gleefully.

"Young lady, you've had too much sugar for your own good. Go ask Maria if she's going to be able to work tonight."

"Come on, I won't tell anyone what you talk about," Sophia protested, clearly understanding the reason her mother was asking her to desert the kitchen for a few moments.

"Sophia," her mother repeated, speaking her daughter's name in a warning manner.

"Okay, but if the sauce burns, it's on you," she said, and then she waved at us both before she exited the kitchen.

"You didn't have to get rid of her on our account," I said.

"Please, she was due for a break when you arrived. This way she and Maria will have a chance to discuss how crazy their mother is." She laughed as she added the last bit.

"I'm sure you're wrong," I protested.

"And I'm just as certain that I'm right. Now, what's this about?"

I had no choice, and yet I still hesitated before I dragged my friend into this. Grace finally coughed and said, "Suzanne, if you don't want to tell her, I'll do it."

"No, I can handle it." I turned to Angelica and asked, "Did you happen to know Annabeth Kline?"

The restaurateur's face saddened instantly. "Of course. I heard about the accident. She dined with us here occasionally, and I was always struck by how alive she seemed. Ironic, isn't it? There's just no way of knowing when an accident will strike someone so vibrant down in the prime of her life."

"That's true enough, but we have reason to believe that what happened to Annabeth was no accident," I explained.

CHAPTER 13

"**S**UZANNE, WHAT ARE YOU TALKING about?" Angelica asked, the concern thick in her voice. "She fell off a ladder in her studio. Everyone knows that."

"Not only does that look unlikely, but we've found a few things that Annabeth left herself saying that she thought someone was trying to kill her. When I got back home, there was a note from her laying it all out." It was an oversimplification of the truth, but there was no reason to go into detail. The gist of it was correct enough. We wouldn't have suspected anything if Annabeth hadn't told us her suspicions herself.

"What do the police say?" Angelica asked.

"We can't go to them with what we've got," I explained. "At least not just yet."

"Stephen Grant is out of town," Grace added.

"But surely he's appointed a substitute in his absence," Angelica countered. "I know you two have solved more than your fair share of crimes in the past, but this seems to require an official investigation, given the circumstances."

"The truth is that we're not sure they're up to it," I said, "and besides, Annabeth didn't exactly come out and give us much in the way of proof. We've been piecing things together and interviewing suspects, all the while trying not to let them know what we're doing."

Angelica nodded. "I understand, then. And Kerry Minter was on her list?"

"No. Yes. Maybe," I said.

"Well, that makes perfect sense," Angelica said as Sophia poked her head back into the kitchen.

"Is it safe to come back in?"

"Two more minutes," Angelica said.

All Sophia did was groan loudly in protest as she quickly exited again.

"Explain," Angelica said she stood and stirred the sauce Sophia had claimed to be worried about. "And eat. Your food is getting cold."

"We can't do both," I protested.

"Speak for yourself," Grace said as she stabbed a forkful of lasagna.

I took a small bite of ravioli, and then I said, "Annabeth had things broken down in a rather odd fashion, and at first glance, it didn't appear that Kerry should be on our list of suspects at all."

"But then you spoke with her in person," Angelica said. "She can be a bit overbearing at times. She fancied herself an artist once upon a time, did you know that? Antonia went to high school with her."

"What happened?" I asked just before I wrapped a little pasta onto my fork.

"She realized that she would never be better than pretty good, and she gave it up," Angelica said, "but I've heard stories that ever since she opened Artie's, she's been more intense than ever. No wonder her business is failing."

"She might have mentioned something about having trouble keeping things afloat, but who isn't these days," I said. "The place was practically empty when we were there earlier."

"I don't doubt it, and I understand she can be abrupt with her customers at times."

"Not all of them," Grace said with a grin after finishing off some of her chicken alfredo.

"You must be talking about Chris Langer," Angelica said from the stove. "Christopho. Hah. When he asked me to call him that the first time, I couldn't keep from grinning for a week. I've known him since he was a boy. Does Kerry *still* have feelings for him? Doesn't she realize that his heart has always belonged to Annabeth?"

"You seem to know a lot about the art world around here," I said.

"What can I say? I have a soft spot for artistic souls," she admitted. "I've even been known to supply their meals on the house occasionally."

That was news to me. I wasn't sure Angelica gave anyone else her friends-and-family discount but us, but then again, why wouldn't she, if it meant that much to her? "So, what are your thoughts?" I asked her as I polished off another bite of linguini.

"You're asking me? You two must be really desperate," she said with a grin.

"We're just getting started," I admitted, "but any insights you have would be greatly appreciated as well as this wonderful food."

"You both should know that you're welcome to anything and everything I have," Angelica said in a grand gesture.

"How about now?" Sophia asked plaintively, this time not daring to do more than stick her head into the kitchen.

Angelica glanced at me, and I nodded that we were finished with the confidential part of our conversation. "Very well," she told her youngest daughter. "By the way, your sauce is fine."

"I'll see about that myself," Sophia said as she took the wooden spoon from her mother and nudged her to one side.

"Do you see how they treat me in my own kitchen?" Angelica asked us with a smile.

"You love it, and you know it," her youngest said. After tasting a bit of it with a clean spoon, she said, "It's perfect."

"There was never any doubt in my mind," Angelica said.

We offered to pay, but we were refused, which didn't really surprise me, given that kitchen meals were considered family time and not customer time. "I'll walk you both out," Angelica said, and after we said our good-byes to the daughters working at the moment, she hesitated at the door. "Suzanne, let me think about your question. May I call you later?"

"Any time, day or night," I said, "though if you can do it before seven at night, that would be great."

Angelica smiled as she patted my cheeks. "I'm well aware of your schedule. It's so good to have you back, my dear."

"It's good to be back, even given the circumstances," I said.

After she was gone, I turned to Grace. "Shall we head back to April Springs now?"

"Not just yet," Grace said.

"We're not going to go speak with Kerry Minter again, are we?" I asked her. "I think we've grilled her quite enough for one day."

"Perhaps, but she's not the only person of interest in Union Square. I'd like a chance to speak with the great Christopho again before we head back, if it's all the same to you."

"I'm game if you are," I said. "I'm not sure where to find him, though."

"I've got that covered. As soon as I found out he was involved in this case, I've been following him on social media, and he just posted that he's working at his studio."

"That's kind of dangerous telling people where he is at all times, isn't it?"

"You'd think so, but there are a quite a few people who seem to revel in it," Grace said.

"Then let's go see him," I agreed.

The artist's studio was in a section of Union Square I hadn't had much opportunity to visit before. Once Momma had insisted I do the art crawl with her there, a special occasion where artists of all types opened their doors to the public in an effort to show off their wares, and hopefully sell something along the way. I'd bought a hook from a blacksmith and a small vase from a potter, but Momma had outdone herself, spending more that evening than I did on food for six months. If we'd seen Christopho's studio, I didn't remember it, but the area was certainly familiar. It had once housed several foundries and warehouses, and studios had been carved out of the spaces, no doubt because it was the cheapest rent the starving artists could find, but it gave the area an artsy feel that was undeniable. The short stretch of studios looked as though it belonged somewhere else, with interesting and colorful murals everywhere, sculptures created from car parts and old appliances on display, and other sundry items that would appeal to even the most bohemian of tastes.

To my surprise, even though it was chilly outside, Christopho's studio door was wide open, propped open by a distinctive rock the size of a baseball that had bits of quartz sticking out at the oddest angles from it. The artist was inside, painting in a short-sleeved shirt and jeans covered by a smock. The easel on the canvas was a mass of bright colors and shapes, and if there was a single recognizable thing represented there, I couldn't spot it. It struck me how different his working conditions were than Annabeth's. Whereas her workspace had been a mess with materials spread out everywhere, evidently Christopho had to

work in a nearly sterile environment, with everything clearly having its own place.

The heat from the place hit me the second we walked in.

"Sorry about the temperature. The communal boiler for this building is on the fritz, and we can't seem to get it regulated," he explained. "Galen's studio is upstairs, so she has to keep the windows open even in the dead of winter. She left ten minutes ago. She said it was too hot to work, and I don't doubt it. What brings you two by? Are you still nosing around in Annabeth's business?"

"I just started following you on social media," Grace said, which was strictly true. "We wanted to talk to you about something that happened at Artie's."

"That scene with Kerry Minter earlier? She's had a crush on me forever. Normally I don't mind, but lately she's been pushing me a bit too hard, and I thought it was time to put a stop to it. Frankly, it's a little embarrassing."

"That's because your heart belonged to Annabeth, didn't it?" I asked him.

He looked pained for a moment before he was able to hide it. "We've already talked about this, ladies. Sure, the two of us were close, but we were just friends. I thought I made that clear to you earlier. Now, if you're not here shopping for art, I'm not sure that there's anything else for us to discuss."

Ignoring his dismissal, I said, "We understand that some pretty heavy boxes just about crushed Annabeth at the art supply store, and that you were one of the people there at the time."

Christopho put his brush down. "I'm surprised Kerry told you about it since she could have been liable if anything had actually happened to Annabeth."

"What makes you think Kerry was the one who told us?" Grace asked.

"Annabeth said something?" he asked. "I was the first one

to get to her. She was a little shaken, but she wasn't hurt. Galen popped out of nowhere a second after I did, and we both managed to calm her down before Kerry showed up."

"I thought she and Galen were blood enemies," I said.

"Most of that was just for show," Christopho said. "Sure, she was jealous of Annabeth's success, but deep down, we were all pulling for each other."

I had a hard time believing that, and I wasn't at all sure if the man himself believed it. Was it possible that he was protecting Galen for some reason?

"So, you didn't have anything to do with those boxes falling, nor did you see who might have. Is that your story?" Grace asked him pointedly.

"It's not a story, it happens to be the truth," he said strongly. There was a fire in his gaze that chilled me a bit. Though he was trying to project the sensitive artist vibe with us, it was obvious that there was a great deal of passion in the man as well.

"Okay, if you say so," Grace said, clearly conceding nothing. "Why Christopho, anyway? Angelica DeAngelis told us you were always Chris growing up. It's a bit pretentious, isn't it?"

What was Grace doing? Was she intentionally trying to get a rise out of the man? If so, she failed to do it this time, though I saw him set his teeth on edge for a moment before he regained control of his temper. "Angelica can call me whatever she wants," he said. "The woman is a saint. As to the name, Chris Langer could be your butcher, but Christopho is clearly an artist." He paused a moment and almost seemed to smile. I hadn't thought the artist was all that handsome until that moment, but there was something about his grin that made him endearing and desirable, at least to a certain type of woman, I supposed. I never cared for the bad-boy bohemian myself, at least not after my brief, tumultuous marriage to Max. When that had been finished, I'd vowed to avoid artistic types at all costs

from there on out, and Jake was the antithesis of that, something that I cherished in him. The artist continued, "If it helps sell paintings, I'm all for it. Was that it? If so, I need to get back to work." I studied the painting, trying to think of something to say about it, but failing miserably. He must have caught my anxiety. "I know what I do isn't to everyone's taste, but I try to capture emotions, not images that could be reproduced with the camera on a cell phone."

"And what emotion does that portray?" I asked as I looked at the swirling masses of dark colors.

"Anger, sadness, and most importantly, loss," he said softly as he stared at his own work.

"So, it's about Annabeth," Grace said softly. "Do I see a touch of regret in there as well?"

He stared straight ahead so long that I thought he might have forgotten us, but after a long and awkward silence, he finally pulled himself out of it. "I've got to get back to work now. Good-bye."

After we left his studio, I said, "Wow, you were on fire in there."

"I'm sorry, but I had to push him," Grace explained.

"I'm not criticizing. That's why we're such a good team. I tend to worry about offending people, but you are absolutely reckless at times," I said. "Don't get me wrong; that's a good thing."

"Did you see the way he reacted when I goaded him? The man might seem all airy and light on the outside, but there's a dark temper running under the surface. Not a lot of women could resist that kind of dangerous magnetism."

"Evidently Annabeth and I were in the minority, then," I said. "How about you?"

"Given different circumstances, I could see having a tryst

with him," she admitted. "That painting he's working on is almost like a confession, isn't it?"

I hadn't seen it that way at all. "What do you mean?"

"If, and at this point I'm saying that all it could be considered is speculation, *if* he killed Annabeth in a fit of passion, his soul is clearly tortured because of it."

I looked at her steadily as we got back into my Jeep. "Did you really see all of that on the canvas? It just looked like one big mess to me."

"I don't know why, but for some reason it spoke to me," she admitted. "He's tortured about her death. There's no doubt about that. But why? Was it from the loss of a love he never attained, or was there something more sinister on the canvas?"

"I have no earthly idea," I admitted. "What did you think about his story about the boxes collapsing at the art supply shop?"

"Wow, he just about lost it when I implied that he might have had something to do with it. I'm not sure if he was responsible or not, but he surely didn't want to talk about it."

As we started back to April Springs, I asked her, "Where did that statement of his that they were all pulling for each other come from?"

"I have no idea, but I don't believe it any more than he does. Maybe he was trying to muddy the waters," Grace asked.

"Why would he want to do that, though? If *he* was the one who killed Annabeth, wouldn't he want us to believe that someone else might have done it instead?"

"I honestly don't know what's going on in that man's mind," Grace admitted.

A few minutes later, I said, "There's another possibility. What if he didn't realize that we're investigating what happened and not just some of Annabeth's friends who miss her? Do you think it's possible that our suspects don't know what we're doing?"

"I'm not sure, but if they don't know by now, they will soon enough."

"Why is that?" I asked her.

"Because we've just about gone beyond what normal people would do, given the situation. They are going to start to suspect that there's a reason we're hanging around asking these probing questions all of a sudden."

"And what happens then?"

"We have to be careful, and at the same time, we need to keep pushing them."

"I agree," I said. "I could be wrong, but I have a strong hunch that we've already spoken with Annabeth's killer today. I'm just not sure which one it was."

"Knowing would certainly make the rest of this easier," Grace said with a nod. "Do you think I pushed Christopho a little bit *too* hard?"

"No," I said firmly. "If you hadn't, we wouldn't have seen the anger in him. Because of that, I can see him lashing out at Annabeth for rejecting him, can't you?"

"Too vividly in my mind," Grace agreed. "Okay, we have a strong motive for Christopho. If Galen killed Annabeth, it may or may not have been jealousy. If Bonnie Small killed her, it could have been because she was leaving her and causing an insurrection on her way out."

"If it was Martin Lancaster, it might have been strictly for a profit on artwork he thought he'd secured, which seems a bit mercenary to me."

"Unless there is more to their story," Grace agreed. "What about Kerry?"

"That one's fairly easy. She's clearly in love with Christopho, but he wanted only Annabeth. With her competition out of the way, she might have thought she was in position to step in and take Annabeth's place."

"Wow, it's kind of unnerving how many different reasons folks might have wanted to see our friend dead, isn't it?" Grace asked.

"Yes, it is. So, where do we go from here?" I asked after stifling a yawn.

"Suzanne, you've had a big day, and we both have a lot to think about. Let's go home and try to forget about it all for tonight," she suggested. "Do you have any interest in a sleepover?"

"Thanks for the offer, but all I want to do is curl up in front of my fireplace, read a bit, and fall asleep. Today has been a huge day, and tomorrow might be even busier."

"I'll accept a rain check, then," Grace said. "Just drop me off at the house on your way."

"It may be *my* bedtime, but I know it's much too early for you. What are you going to do?"

"I may be on vacation, but that doesn't mean I can just ignore the paperwork that seems to pile up in my job more and more every day. I'll slog through some of that. Nothing is more certain to knock me out than that."

"You still love what you do though, right?" I asked her.

"Nearly as much as you love Donut Hearts," she said with a smile.

CHAPTER 14

WHEN I WALKED THROUGH THE front door of the cottage, my cell phone started to ring. If it was Jake, it was perfect timing.

Too bad it wasn't.

"Hello, Suzanne. It's Alyssa."

"Hi, Alyssa. What's up? I know I said I was going to check in with you, but I thought Grace and I would come by tomorrow after I finish up at the donut shop. Would that be okay?" I understood her desire for updates on our progress, but I was flat worn out, and I didn't really want to rehash everything we'd learned that afternoon without getting a chance to mull it all over or, better yet, talk to Jake about it. I'd been going back and forth about telling him my suspicions about what had really happened to Annabeth, but I had a hunch that the second I heard his voice, I was going to spill it all.

"That's not why I'm phoning you," Alyssa said. "Oh, my goodness! I just realized the time! You must go to work at the donut shop awfully early."

"I get there at three a.m. every day," I explained.

"I'm so sorry. Please forget I even called. This can wait," she said as she started to hang up.

"Hold on. I have a few minutes before I have to go to bed."

"Are you sure?"

"I'm positive," I replied. It was clear that she wasn't all that eager to tell me what was on her mind, which was just one more

reason to press her while she was interested in talking to me about whatever it was that was clearly troubling her.

"I thought of something you might misinterpret if you discover it first yourself, and I wanted to get out in front of it, so I could explain it to you," she said.

This sounded bad. What on earth was the woman talking about? "Go on. I'm listening," I said.

"Annabeth loaned me a rather large sum of money a few days before she died," Alyssa said as the words seemed to gush out of her.

"Let me guess; it was ten thousand dollars, wasn't it?"

After an elongated pause, she said, "You found it, then."

"We did, but we didn't know what it was for," I said. "We thought somebody might be blackmailing her."

"Heavens no. What would anyone have on my daughter to be able to blackmail her? No, don't answer that. Let me explain."

"It's not important. Just knowing where the money went is all that we really need to know."

"It's important to me!" she said firmly.

"Okay." I wasn't about to try to stop her.

"Suzanne, I haven't always made the best choices. I listened to an investment counselor who ended up crippling me financially. He made his commissions and fees, all right, but I'm the one who lost a fortune. I was trying to get myself back on my feet after I fired him when Annabeth figured out what was going on. She offered to loan me enough money until I could figure things out, but I refused. That didn't stop her, though. She pulled the cash out of her account without my knowledge and presented it to me as a done deal. She wanted me to forget about paying her back, claiming that she owed me at least that much on studio rental space, but I wouldn't hear of it. It took some haggling on my part, but I finally got her to agree to allow me to pay it back at the current interest rate banks paid on super savings accounts.

I wanted to pay her full interest on the loan at the same rate the bank would charge me, but she wouldn't agree to that, so we finally came to a meeting of the minds. I feel so awful about it now I just want to cry."

"Alyssa, *everybody* gets in trouble at one point or another in their lives," I told her, thinking about some of the boneheaded moves I'd made in my own life. They weren't so much financial as personal, but marrying Max had been a matter of misplaced trust as well, so maybe we weren't all that different after all.

"At my age, I should have known better. He told me things that were too good to be true, and I believed him."

"It sounds as though Annabeth understood all of that," I said.

"She said she did, but it was humiliating having to go to her with my woes. Parents are supposed to take care of their children, not the other way around." The woman sounded so defeated I felt bad for her.

"If my mother and I were in the same situation and I had the money to spare, I wouldn't have hesitated for a second to do the same thing Annabeth did," I told her firmly and with full conviction. "She had the money to spare, right?"

"Oh, yes. She was doing quite well with her art and her logo business as of late," she admitted. "That still doesn't make any of this any easier."

"There is no doubt in my mind that she was thrilled to have the opportunity to do it."

"You're kind to say so," Alyssa acknowledged meekly.

"It's not just lip service, Alyssa. I mean it, and I'm sure Annabeth was more than happy to be able to help."

"She seemed to be," she admitted. "Anyway, I thought you should know. How is it going? No, strike that. We'll talk about it tomorrow. Have a good night's sleep, Suzanne."

"You do the same," I said.

After we hung up, I built a fire and started thinking about money. I'd seen firsthand how the lust for it could drive people to do the most horrid things, but I'd also seen where it had been used for good. I firmly believed that money itself wasn't inherently evil, but a driving desire to acquire more and more of it had ruined more lives than I even wanted to think about. I was just happy that it had never been that much of a motivating factor in my own life. It wasn't that I didn't always feel I could use more of the green stuff, but I didn't let it rule my life, either.

I was still thinking about that when my cell phone rang again.

This time it was my dear, sweet husband, calling at exactly the right time to cheer me up and bring me out of the funk I'd let my conversation with Alyssa put me in.

"Hey there, stranger," he said. "I miss you."

"I miss you, too. How's it going in Tennessee?" I asked.

"Just getting into it now," Jake admitted. By the terse way he spoke, I knew that he wasn't ready to discuss it with me. My husband liked to take in the facts and let them percolate before he dove into action if the circumstances allowed it. Me, I was a jump-straight-into-the-pool kind of gal, so we complemented each other. "How are you doing really? Getting back into your old life okay?"

"More than you know," I said, trying to keep my tone light.

"Suzanne, what have you been up to?"

"What do you mean?" I asked as innocently as I could manage.

"I know you, young lady. You're getting involved in more than just donuts, aren't you?"

"Jake, somebody killed Annabeth. Her death was no accident, and Grace and I are going to prove it."

"Tell me all about it," he said, not questioning whether I should be investigating or not or even the conclusion Grace and I had reached about Annabeth's demise.

"First of all, the ladder appeared to have been tampered with, but that's not all. Based on where they found the body, she *couldn't* have fallen. I checked out the angles myself. Someone must have hit her from behind and then staged it to look as though it was an accident."

"You were in her *studio*?" he asked curiously. "Why were you even there?"

"I went to pay my respects to Alyssa, and while I was there—Grace was with me, too—she asked us to look around and make sure everything was all right. That's not what got us started believing that her death was deliberate, though. Do you remember the painting she did for me?"

"The one that Emma brought over from the cottage? Sure. What about it?"

"There was a note inside written in our old high school code saying that someone was trying to kill her, and the inside of the brown paper had lots of clues as to who it might have been. She *knew* someone was targeting her. She just didn't have a name yet."

"Who's on your list of suspects so far?" Jake asked.

"Let's see. We've got an artist named Galen, a competitor of Annabeth's on the local art scene who was extremely jealous of her, a man named Christopho, well, Chris really, who she continually spurned, a seedy agent named Bonnie Small she was getting ready to fire, a gallery owner who wants to capitalize on Annabeth's death in the worst way, and an art supply store owner who was jealous of the way Christopho felt about her."

"Wow, you've certainly accomplished a lot since I've been gone," he said, the admiration clear in his voice.

"Don't forget, Grace was helping me, too," I admitted.

"I'm sure she did, but we both know that *you're* the driving force when it comes to your investigations. What else have you learned?"

After covering a few more pieces of background about the case, I went on to explain, "Annabeth believed that someone tried to push a wall of heavy boxes on top of her at the art store, and she said something about a possible assault by automobile in front of the art gallery. Lastly, she claimed that she realized someone had been messing with the ladder of her studio. You know what? That part sort of clears Bonnie Small, her agent. She's been trying to get into that studio by hook and by crook, but she's been thwarted at every time. If she had a key, she could have just waltzed right in and taken everything she wanted to.

"Unless she just wants you to believe that she doesn't have one," Jake said. "Just how clever is she?"

"Well, she managed to convince a handful of artists that *they* needed *her*," I admitted, "though she was beginning to hemorrhage clients when Annabeth died."

"So, she's smart enough to make things complicated," Jake opined.

"Yes, she probably is," I reluctantly admitted. "Then she's not off the list after all."

"It's early in your investigation yet, Suzanne. You know how these things can take time."

"I do, but that doesn't mean that I have to like it," I said in response. "The truth is, it's lonely here without you."

"I know. I feel the same way," he said. "I'm kind of surprised Grace isn't over there with you. I figured the two of you would be having sleepovers while I'm away."

"She suggested it, as a matter of fact," I said, "but I wasn't in the mood for company. You know what I mean."

"I do," he said. "Listen, I might be able to get out of this if

you want me to try. I just got here yesterday, so I don't think it would be a problem. I'm sure Tommy can find someone else."

"Someone as good as you?" I asked him.

"Probably. I'm not as special as you think I am, though I love that you do," he said.

"We both know better than that. Jake, I need to do this with Grace. We're being careful. Shoot, I'm willing to bet that our suspects don't even realize yet that we know Annabeth was murdered."

"The key word in that sentence is *yet*," Jake answered. "If you keep digging into this, which I'm certain both of you are going to do, they're going to see what you're up to soon enough."

"We'll be even more careful then," I said. "Don't worry about us. We'll be fine."

"Easier said than done, I'm afraid," he answered. "Listen, the offer stands. If you change your mind, I'm just a phone call away."

"And hundreds of miles," I added.

"Sure, but that's just logistics. We can work that out. I mean it, Suzanne."

"I know you do, and I take great comfort in the fact. Just promise me you won't come home yet. I need this."

"You've got my word," he said. "So, besides that, how else have things been going since you've been back? How does it feel working at Donut Hearts again?"

"Better than I could even imagine," I said with a smile, even though he couldn't see me.

"I'm glad to hear that."

"I still miss you, though," I added quickly.

"I get that, but you need to get your old life back, even if it means risking it digging into another murder. Just be careful."

"Always," I said.

"Let's agree to disagree on that one," he said with a slight

chuckle in his voice. "Listen, I won't keep you, I know it's getting to be past your bedtime."

"I can make an exception if it means I get to stay up and talk to you," I said.

"Yes, but you'll pay for it in the morning, and we both know it."

"Any last-minute suggestions?" I asked him. I was feeling a little unsure of myself, given how my last investigation had ended up. I'd nearly gotten killed by someone who had barely registered on the radar of my investigation, so I wasn't so sure that I hadn't lost my touch for sleuthing completely.

"I'd say 'follow the money,' but it appears that there are a different set of motives than that at work here," he admitted. "I suppose the real question is who had the most to gain by her death? Who had access to that studio? According to what you told me earlier, she wouldn't let just anyone waltz in there. Do any of your suspects have alibis for the time of the murder? Is there any reason one of them couldn't have done it physically? It's not as easy to kill someone from behind with a single blow as they make it look on television. Who was she meeting behind the library after hours, and why? Do all of your suspects have alibis for that meeting as well? Those questions should at least get you thinking in the right direction."

I had to whistle loudly at my husband's ad-libbed list of insightful questions. "I've said it before, and I'll say it again. You must have been one heck of a cop back in the day, sir."

"I had my moments, but don't sell yourself short. I'm sure you'll come up with the right answer in the end."

"I just wish I had the faith in myself that you have in me."

"Don't worry about that. I've got enough for both of us!"

"Good. I need all of it I can get," I said, and then, after exchanging our loves and good nights, I hooked my cell phone up to its charger, curled up on the couch, and went straight to

sleep. I might have had a great deal on my mind dealing with Annabeth's murder, but there was nothing I could do about it at the moment, and if I was going to start making donuts again soon, I needed to get all of the rest I could. As I snuggled up in front of the fire, still covered from head to toe in a toasty blanket as well, I decided I was going to keep sleeping out there until Jake came home. It was just too lonely in that big old bed all by myself.

Besides, some of my best sleeps had taken place right where I was at the moment. When I'd been a little girl, Momma and Daddy had let me bunk out there and watch the fire on special occasions. I could still remember one year during the heart of a giant snowstorm with the curtains all pulled aside so I could watch the dancing fire and the swirling snow at the same time, alone with my thoughts, but feeling safe and warm with my folks just footsteps away. To this day, it's one of my most precious childhood memories, and that was what I basked in as sleep took me over, and I dreamed happy thoughts and, for at least the moment, left our quest for a killer far behind me.

CHAPTER 15

I T FELT GOOD GETTING MY hands dirty again—if you can call making batter and dough dirty work. Some folks might have thought so, but not me. It was a tranquil time for me, the mornings I worked in the shop alone. I hadn't always wanted to be a donut maker, but it turned out that it had been exactly what I'd needed when Max had cheated on me and wrecked our marriage. I'd rebuilt my life with my divorce settlement, buying Donut Hearts and moving back in with Momma in the cottage I now shared with Jake, and these days I couldn't imagine my life any other way.

As I separated the batter for the day's cake donuts into several different bowls so I could mix up different flavors, I had to smile. This was where I belonged.

To my surprise, as I was pulling the last banana-peanut butter-chocolate chip cake donuts out of the oil, I heard the front door open.

Picking up the heavy donut dropper from the sink, remnants of the last batter still clinging to its sides, I walked carefully out front, ready to use it as a weapon if I needed to.

"Emma, what are you doing here?" I asked my assistant as she hung up her coat.

"I couldn't sleep, so I thought I'd come in today and work, if you don't mind," she said. "I got so used to working seven days a week that it was nearly impossible for me to take a day off. You don't mind, do you?"

There was a tinge of sadness in my heart, since I'd been looking forward to another day working alone, but I quickly buried it and put on my best smile. "Of course. I'd love the company," I said.

"Were you going to attack me with that dropper?" she asked with a grin as she pointed to my hand.

"Well, I wasn't going to offer you a treat, but since it's just you, would you like to taste one of my latest creations after I ice them?"

"What are they? They certainly smell intriguing," she said.

"I was reading a biography of Elvis while I was recovering, and I kept wondering why I didn't try something in his honor. My college roommate's stepmother was a huge fan of the man, and when he did three shows in her home town of Charleston, West Virginia, she went to all three shows. Apparently Elvis loved peanut butter and banana sandwiches."

"And the chocolate chips?" she asked as we walked back into the kitchen together and she examined one of the unglazed donuts a little more closely.

"Those are all me," I admitted as I rearranged the donuts on the icing tray and gave them a solid coating before serving one to Emma. "I read that he added bacon to his sandwiches sometimes, but I didn't have any on hand, so I thought I'd add some sweetness instead."

Emma took a bite, and I joined her, eating the other half of the donut she was sampling. "It's pretty good," she said.

"Yes, but there's still something missing. Maybe I *will* try to add some bacon next time."

"You're not chucking these out though, are you?" she asked. "My dad would love them just the way they are."

"Then by all means, bag a couple and take them home to him," I said.

"I would, but I'm not living there anymore," she admitted a bit warily.

"What? You moved out? Are you living with Barton?" I knew that my assistant and the chef were getting close, but I hadn't realized they were at that stage yet.

"No, I'm kind of an old-fashioned girl. Unless and until we're married, I'm not going to live with him. I found a place on campus. It just got to be too much living with my folks at my age."

"I suppose, but remember, I lived with Momma into my thirties," I said with a grin.

"I know, but those were extenuating circumstances," she said.

"How do your folks feel about it?"

"Mom's okay with it, but Dad has been loading me down with so many self-defense whistles, pepper spray, brass knuckles, and other things, I can't even carry a regular purse anymore. My new place is close to campus and only a twenty-minute commute here. Are you okay with it, Suzanne?"

"Why wouldn't I be? If you're happy, then it was the right decision," I said.

"Oh, I'm delirious," she replied. "I'm ten minutes closer to Barton, I can get to my classes in a flash, and I love being independent. I have three roommates, and they're all really special ladies."

"I'm thrilled for you, then," I said.

For some reason, she looked happy to hear the news. Did my opinion really matter that much to her? Emma was more than just an employee, she was my friend, but it was still nice to know that she cared about what I thought.

She smiled as she said, "You get started on the yeast donuts, and I'll jump on those dishes. Believe it or not, I've missed burying my arms up to my elbows in warm soapy water and

worrying about nothing more than getting the pots and pans sparkling clean."

"It's quite a responsibility running things, isn't it? I can't thank you enough for stepping in the way you did."

"I was happy to do it. In fact, if I hadn't had the opportunity, I never could have afforded my new place, so I should be the one thanking you."

As I measured out the ingredients for my yeast donuts and added them to my massive stand mixer, I found myself at peace like I'd never achieved being away.

There were only two things that could have made my life better: Jake would have been with me, and Annabeth Kline would still be alive.

During our break, we took the time to catch up more outside, though it was freezing out. It was a tradition Emma and I kept up from the heat of summer to the frigid temperatures of winter and all points between. We didn't necessarily linger since it was well below freezing outside, but those few minutes of fresh air revived me more than a hot shower and a cup of coffee ever could.

With the donuts made and stowed carefully in our display cases, I was ready to open Donut Hearts' doors for the day. I knew I wasn't going to get the same kind of crowd that I'd gotten the day before, but I was still surprised to find only one customer waiting to get in, if in fact he was a customer at all.

"Martin, what brings you by the donut shop so early?" I asked the art gallery owner as I let him into the warm shop.

"I've heard about your donuts, and I wanted to try one for

myself," he said as he rubbed his hands together. "What do you recommend?"

"That's hard to say," I told him as I took my place behind the counter. "It's like asking the mother of a dozen kids which one is her favorite."

"Does anyone really have twelve children anymore?" he asked incredulously.

"It's been known to happen," I said.

"Just give me one of those," he said as he pointed to a plain glazed yeast donut, the most innocuous of the donuts I served. Even the plain cake had more texture and flavor, not that the glazed was inferior in any way. There was just no sizzle, no pizzazz to it.

"Coffee as well?" I asked.

"No, just the donut," he said.

I plated it up for him and slid it in front of him. After collecting the pittance I charged for a single donut, I said, "If you need anything else, don't hesitate to ask."

"Actually, there was one other thing," he replied.

"We have hot chocolate, too," I suggested.

"No, it has nothing to do with your business, however good your treats might be."

"You wouldn't know that though, would you?" I asked him sweetly. "You haven't even tasted the one you just bought."

"Oh, of course," he said, and then the gallery owner took a small bite. The look of surprise on his face was sincere.

"Do you like it?"

"It's the best donut I've ever had in my life," he said, as if it were the greatest shock he'd ever had.

"Thanks," I said. "They're made by hand right on the spot, fresh every morning, using only the finest ingredients."

"I can tell," he said, and then he took another bite. In a few moments, he'd finished it. "Three more, please."

"Would you like them to go?" I asked.

"No, I'll eat them right here. And maybe throw in some of that hot chocolate, too." He tossed a five-dollar bill down on the counter, and I gave him his change after I served him again. "These really are amazing," he said, clearly surprised that the second donut was as good as the first one.

"I'm glad you approve," I said. I was starting to like this man more and more by the minute. Maybe I'd just caught him at a bad time before.

"Now, about that painting Annabeth gave you," he said.

"Which one?"

"You have more than one?" he asked eagerly. "That's the best news I've had in days. I want them all."

"I'm sorry," I said.

"I don't expect you to give them away, Suzanne, but I'd like to buy them from you." He pulled out what appeared to be a business checkbook. "Just name your price."

"Sight unseen?" I asked him. "How can you agree to a price if you don't know what you're buying?"

"I've seen enough of Annabeth's work to be able to make you a generous offer," he said.

"Sorry, but they aren't for sale," I said flatly. Wow, he'd gone from my Nice to Naughty list in record time.

"Come now, we are both professionals. *Everything* has a price."

"I suppose I might settle for one million dollars," I said.

"That's a ridiculous price to set for a group of paintings from a relatively unknown artist," he said dismissively. "While it's true that Annabeth's works have increased substantially in value since her passing, they aren't worth anything near what you're asking. After all, you don't expect me to forego a reasonable profit myself, do you?"

"I'm sorry. You misunderstood me."

"I was hoping that was the case," he said, easing up a bit.

"It's a million apiece," I said.

"No one is going to give you that for her work," he argued.

"That's exactly why I named that price. I'm not selling *anything* I got from Annabeth, and that's final. There's not enough money in the world."

Lancaster frowned for a few moments, and then he nodded. "I can see that. May I at least see them? I can join you whenever it's convenient for you, as long as it's today or tomorrow."

"Sorry, but I'm not sure that's such a good idea," I said.

"Why not, if I may ask?"

"My schedule is pretty full for the next few weeks," I said. "I just don't think I can get away."

"Do you at least have photos of them on your cell phone?" he asked, pushing me a little harder than I thought he should have.

I was about to admit that I did have some of the images, but something made me hold back. Maybe it was that he was just a little too eager. "I can't help you."

"Very well," he said, pushing his unfinished plate of donuts away. "If you change your mind, you know where to find me."

"I do, but I won't," I said. "Would you like what's left to go?"

"No, I've had my fill," he said as he stood.

Before he could go, I knew I had another question to ask him, and I might not get a chance if he took offense at my refusal of his request. "I heard about the car incident at your gallery involving Annabeth."

"That was nothing," he said, and then he stared at me for a moment before asking, "What exactly have you heard?"

"Just that Annabeth thought it was more than nothing," I said as cryptically as I could manage.

"I'm certain that it was nothing more than a teenager texting while he was behind the wheel of some little red car, and he

clearly didn't see her crossing the road. Annabeth was talking to me when it happened, so she didn't spot him until it was nearly too late. I'm the one who warned her and pulled her out of its path, for goodness sake."

"Are you *sure* it was a teenager behind the wheel?" I asked him.

"Who knows with these darkly tinted windows in some of the cars these days? I just assume that was what happened."

"Do any of your clients happen to *own* red cars?" I asked.

"How should I know?" he asked dismissively. "By any chance, do you know anyone else who might own some of Annabeth's works?"

"Sorry, not a soul," I lied. I knew Momma had purchased several pieces over the years, but she was even more sentimental than I was, though she was loath to admit it. He had as much chance of persuading Momma to sell as he did to talk Max into shaving his head, and for anyone who knew my ex-husband, they would realize how impossible that task would be.

"Very well," he said. "If you hear of anyone or if you change your own mind, please be sure to let me know."

"I will," I said. Maybe I'd been a little too rash shutting him down so quickly. After all, if I dangled a possible piece of artwork for sale in front of him, he'd have no choice but to talk to me. I decided to put that on the back burner for now. In the meantime, it had been a curious conversation, and I mulled it over quite a bit over the few hours as I waited on my customers. The number of folks coming in to buy donuts was still pretty high, but I couldn't imagine the trend would continue for much longer. After all, I was back in April Springs with no intention of going anywhere, so the newness of my return was bound to wear off soon enough.

In the meantime, I still managed to find the time to consider the possibilities of the case. We'd eliminated the leads about

the large withdrawal Annabeth had made, the mysterious phone number, and there was something about Martin Lancaster's story that had a ring of truth in it. The boxes nearly hitting Annabeth was still a viable attempt to at least scare her off if not kill her, the car might or might not have been accidental, and there was still that late-night meeting behind the library to consider. Those, with the fact that someone had come into her studio, an exclusive club if ever there was one, were all strong factors in our case. The motives she'd listed could be at issue, but they each had their own strong ties with our remaining list of suspects. Grace and I hadn't been able to nibble away at that yet, and I knew that needed to be our priority after I closed the donut shop for the day. I knew that coming out and asking Martin Lancaster, Galen, Christopho, Bonnie Small, and Kerry Minter directly for alibis would make them *all* suspicious, but at this point, it couldn't be helped.

We needed to narrow down our list to make it more workable. After all, at least *one* of them had to have had an alibi.

I hoped so, at any rate.

I finally realized that it was time to stop being coy and be more direct with our questions. I knew Grace wasn't going to have a problem with that line of attack, and I was going to be glad to sit back and watch her go after the people on our list.

At least I wouldn't have to confront them directly by myself.

Or so I thought at the time.

CHAPTER 16

"J AKE? WHAT'S UP?" IT WAS a little before ten a.m., and I couldn't imagine why my husband was calling me. For one thing, he was presumably busy with his new client, and for another, he knew that I was working. "Is something wrong?"

"That depends on how you look at it," he said a little oddly.

"How do *you* look at it?"

"Let me ask you a question," he said after pausing for a few moments. "How would you feel about me coming home? I know I promised I wouldn't, but the circumstances here have changed."

"I'd love it. You don't even have to ask. But I thought you were busy."

"I thought so, too," he admitted. "But apparently my schedule has just opened up."

"What happened? Did you get *fired*?" I asked him. I couldn't imagine the circumstances under which that could happen, but then again, I couldn't foresee *any* conditions where he'd leave a job once he'd agreed to take it on. "No, that can't be it."

"The truth is that Tommy and I had a difference of opinion," Jake said. "He wanted to use our client as bait to catch the woman in the act of trying to kill him. I couldn't agree to that in a million years. Suzanne, it wouldn't have just put *our* lives at risk unnecessarily, but it would jeopardize the man who was trusting us to *protect* him. I started to go to our employer to tell

him just that when Tommy overruled me, and he told me that it was his way or the highway."

"So you chose the highway," I said.

"I'm on it right now, as a matter of fact," Jake answered. "I should be there sometime this evening, if that suits you."

"You bet it does, but Jake, aren't you still worried about the man you were hired to protect?"

"Suzanne, he wouldn't listen to me, either! I called him the moment Tommy fired me, but he said he had to trust the man he'd hired to do the job. I did everything I could, but if nobody will listen to me, my hands are tied. I hate leaving things like that, and you know it, but what else could I do? Start tailing him until I got arrested for stalking him instead of this lunatic he used to date? There was no way I could help, so I'm washing my hands of the whole mess. You know, I'm not sure I'm cut out for this kind of work after all."

"You've had some good experiences, too," I reminded him.

"I understand that, but it takes just one bad one to taint the rest of them. Don't worry, I'll come up with something to do with my time. How goes your investigation?"

"We're spinning our wheels at the moment, but I have high hopes that we'll make some progress soon," I said. That's all that it was, hope, but it didn't cost a thing to wish.

"I'm sure you will, and if you need me, I'll be more than happy to help as soon as I get back."

"I thought you just said that you were finished with that kind of work," I reminded him, trying my best to make him smile over the line.

I must have succeeded, because I swore I could hear his smile in his voice when he responded. "When I do *those* jobs, I get paid," he said. "This is different."

"Hey, *I* pay you. It's just not something you could declare on your taxes," I said, happy that, no matter what the reason, my

husband was on his way home to me. It may have been selfish of me, but I didn't care. I knew if Jake said that he'd done all he could to make things work out, it was the unvarnished truth.

"That's too true," he said. "Hey, do you know why Phillip would be calling me?"

"I don't have a clue," I admitted.

"Well, I'd better take it. It might be important, and besides, I'll let you get back to work. I just wanted to touch base with you and tell you what was going on."

"I appreciate that," I said.

Once we hung up, I found myself feeling better, and not just about the case. Having Jake around was important to my peace of mind, and I hoped he felt the same way about me.

Ten minutes later, the mayor walked in. "Why, if it isn't George Morris himself. I feel special. That's two visits from you in two days."

"You should be honored," he said with a grin. "I was sitting in my office wondering how I ever let myself be talked into being the mayor of our fair city, and that made me think of you."

"Hey, don't blame me. It was all Momma's doing, remember?" I recalled how she'd orchestrated a write-in campaign for George when she'd no longer been interested in the job, and he'd taken over the reins of our fair town, albeit reluctantly. It had turned out to be a stroke of genius, though. George was a better mayor than anyone, with the possible exception of my mother, could have ever imagined.

"I know full well who was responsible," he said. "I don't exactly regret taking the job, but I do miss our investigations. It was fun working with you once upon a time."

"Including getting injured on the job?" I asked him, recalling

the time when he'd been assaulted in the line of duty all because he'd been working with me.

"Hey, if there weren't any risks, it just wouldn't be any fun," he said, patting his once-bad leg. "Anyway, I've bounced back from that all of the way, so if you need me, you know where to find me."

"Thanks, George. That means a lot to me."

"Well, that's all I wanted to say," he told me. "I'd better get back to the office. I've been ducking Lem Enright all morning, but I have to talk to him sooner or later, so I might as well get it over with."

"Trouble at city hall?" I asked him.

"Nothing I can't handle," he said with a grin.

"Hang on a second," I said as I grabbed an old-fashioned cake donut, one of his favorites, and chucked it in a bag. "For the road."

"I shouldn't," he said as he peeled a dollar off the wad in his pocket.

"Sorry, but I can't take back free samples," I said, refusing his bill. "Thanks for stopping by, though, and be sure to come again."

He looked as though he wanted to fight me on it, but ultimately, George changed his mind. "It was my pleasure. Remember what I said, Suzanne. I'm never more than a phone call away."

"I'm counting on it," I said, smiling as the mayor left. George and I had been friends for years, and it was always good to see him. I'd missed being around the people I cared about when I'd been gone, and I swore to myself that I'd never willingly run away again. This was where I belonged, and I wasn't about to let a little thing like a nearly successful attempt on my life drive me off anymore.

I'd sent Emma on her way at closing time, but I wasn't quite ready to leave the shop myself. The truth was that I needed a little quiet time at Donut Hearts without her, though I would have never come out and said it to anyone else. For some reason, the transition back to my old life was harder with anyone else around. I suppose some of it could have been because when I envisioned this day during my rehab, I was always working alone, at least initially.

There was a tap on the front door as I finished up the deposit slip, and as I looked up, I expected to find Grace standing there waiting for me to let her in. Well, she was there all right, but she wasn't alone, and that did surprise me.

Momma and Phillip were there with her, too.

"Come on in, guys," I said as I let them in and locked the door behind them. "I didn't realize we were having a party, but I have a dozen donuts I can contribute."

"Suzanne, we need to talk to you," Grace said solemnly, not matching my jovial mood.

"This isn't an intervention or something, is it?" I asked them, wondering what the three of them could possibly want to speak with me together for.

"No, it's nothing like that," Momma said with a raised eyebrow. She then turned to Grace. "Go on. Don't keep her waiting. Tell her."

"Suzanne, I hate to do this to you, but I've suddenly been called in to work. I'm going to have to bail on you."

"That happens," I said with a bit of alarm in my voice. "Is there something else going on here that you're not telling me?"

"No, but it kills me to leave you in the middle of an investigation," she said.

149

"That's why we're here," Phillip said with a smile. "We're going to fill in for her."

"As much as I appreciate the offer, Jake's going to be home this evening," I said.

"I know, I called him about a cold case I'm working on, and he told me what happened. Good for him. I don't blame him a bit for leaving a bad situation he couldn't make any better by staying."

"I'm sure he would appreciate that," I said, "but I've got this covered."

"You're not doing this alone, even for eight hours," Momma said emphatically. "That's that."

"Nothing's going to happen to me," I assured her.

From the expression on her face, I knew that I was wasting my breath. "Nonetheless, we are at your service." She turned to Grace. "Don't worry, dear. We'll be fine."

"I know that," she admitted. "I just don't want to miss out on any of the fun."

"I'll keep you informed," I said as I hugged her. "If you'd like, I could call you tonight and give you a progress report."

"Thanks, I appreciate that. Are you sure you'll be okay?" she asked softly as she hugged me.

"I'll be just dandy," I said with a grin. "Now go."

"Okay. I can't believe they are calling me back in on my vacation. There's one silver lining to it, though."

"That we're here to help in your place?" Phillip asked. It was clear he was chomping at the bit to get back into action.

"Sure, but I also get double the time off later," she said. "You three stay safe, do you hear me? There's a killer out there who's not going to like what you're doing, and if you get as aggressive as you're going to need to be to get some solid answers, whoever killed Annabeth is going to know that you're on their trail."

"We'll be careful," I said. "Are you headed to Charlotte?"

"To the airport, anyway. I'm headed out to the west coast. Evidently one of my bosses has resigned suddenly, and my input is required on her replacement."

A sense of dread swept through me suddenly. "They aren't going to make you take her place out there, are they?" The thought of losing my best friend from my everyday life was almost too much to bear.

"No, they know better. I refuse to climb any higher up the corporate ladder if I have anything to say about it. Why in the world would I leave the sweet gig I've got going right now?" She glanced at her watch. "I've got to hustle if I'm going to make my flight."

"Save travels, child," Momma told her and then added a hug of her own before Grace could leave. Phillip smiled and waved, and I watched in silence as Grace took off headed for the sky.

"Don't worry about bringing us up to speed. We've been briefed," Phillip said as soon as I turned back to them. "Do you have a game plan going forward, or do we need to put our heads together and come up with something? We're not rookies, you know. Not only was I a cop for a great many years, but your mother and I have worked cases with you before."

He didn't have to remind me. This was getting to be a Greatest Hits Tour with Grace, Phillip, Momma, and soon Jake helping with an investigation. George had offered his services as well, and as far as I knew, I might be calling on him at some point, too. It might even take every last one of them to get to the truth, but if that's what it took, then that was what I was willing to do.

"I don't know about you two, but I'm kind of hungry," I told them. "Is there any chance we can stop by for a bite to eat at the Boxcar before we start sleuthing?"

"I could eat," Phillip said as he patted his stomach. He'd lost so much weight since I'd been gone that I didn't think one of Trish's meals would hurt him. "How about you, Dot?"

"Actually, it sounds delightful," Momma agreed. "I understand they have a new soup-and-sandwich combination that I've been dying to try. I just can't find a decent broccoli-and-cheese soup these days."

"Then let's go," I said.

CHAPTER 17

"**H**EY, GANG," TRISH SAID AS she greeted us the moment we walked into the Boxcar Grill. I loved that she had remodeled old train cars to make a restaurant, including the kitchen and dining rooms, and it didn't hurt that the food was great and that it was so close to my cottage and my place of work that I could eat there just about whenever I took a hankering for it. "It looks like I'm getting the whole clan, less Jake. Where's Grace?" she asked as she watched the door behind us.

"She got called to the west coast," I said. "Right now she's on her way to the airport."

"That girl is a real jet-setter, isn't she?"

"Do you envy that?" Momma asked her.

"No, ma'am. I *love* knowing where I'm going to be every day and what I'll be doing. Some folks might think of it as being in a rut, but it's what makes me happy. I've got my diner, Suzanne has her donut shop, you have your business interests, and Phillip is solving cases from the past that everyone else gave up on long ago. It's important to feel productive, isn't it?"

"I believe it's one of the keys to a long and happy life," Momma said. "Any chance broccoli-and-cheese soup is on the menu today?"

"You're in luck," Trish said. "Lately we serve it only on days that end in 'y.'"

"Does that mean that there's no variety through the week?" Phillip asked. "I've never been a big fan of broccoli."

"Until Hilda learns to make smaller batches of soup, I'm afraid that's all we're going to be offering for the foreseeable future," she said with a grin.

"Well, I'll do my part to lessen the surplus," Momma said.

"You folks find a table, and I'll be right with you," Trish said as Sandy White and her son, Thomas, presented their bill to pay.

"Don't rush on our accounts," Sandy said. "Hey, folks. How are you? Suzanne, it's so good to have you back."

"It's good to be back," I told my friend and loyal customer. "How have you been?"

"He's growing like a weed, isn't he?" she asked with a smile as she rubbed her son's head.

"Mo-o-mm," he protested.

"Wha-a-t?" she asked, mocking his inflection.

"I'll see you two later," I said with a smile. Sandy, her best friend, Terri, as well as five or six dozen other folks made me glad that I'd stayed in April Springs.

Once we had our table, Phillip took his time perusing the menu. "Why do you insist on doing that?" Momma asked her husband with mock disdain. "You know what you're going to get. It never fails that you order the same thing every time we eat here. For the past eight times we've been here, you've gotten a club sandwich, no tomato, French fries, and sweet tea."

"You never know. I might just fool you one of these days," he said as he continued to study the menu, squinting a bit as he read the fine print.

"Glasses, Phillip," Momma reminded him.

He sheepishly pulled out a pair and put them on. "You're right. That's much better."

"I'm glad," she said, and then she turned to me. "Now, while

154

he's deciding on his next exotic choice, let's chat. It must have been hard to learn that Annabeth's death wasn't an accident after all."

"We're still not one hundred percent sure," I said, hedging my bets a little. After all, it was possible that my friend had been paranoid in the notes she'd left me, though the positioning of that ladder would bother me until I could prove that she hadn't fallen from it, and there were just too many people who wished her ill.

"What does your gut tell you, though?" Momma asked.

"That she was killed by someone else. There's no doubt about it."

"Then that's the premise we work from. Have you spoken with Alyssa about your theory?" she asked carefully.

"She agrees with us," I said. "As a matter of fact, she's doing everything in her power to aid in our investigation."

"And why wouldn't she?" Momma asked softly. "If our positions were reversed, I would never sleep until I brought your assailant to justice."

"Same here," I said as I patted her hand lovingly.

Trish approached the table with three sweet teas on a tray. Momma looked at her with amusement clear on her face. "I'm sorry, I must have blacked out there for a moment. Did we already order our drinks?"

"No, ma'am, but if you'd like something else, I'd be happy to fetch it," Trish said with a grin. She was one of the few folks in the world that my mother didn't intimidate. Most of the time, anyway.

Momma smiled openly at her. "What can I say? You've called my bluff. I'd adore some of your sweet tea."

"I would, too," I said. "Phillip?"

"Yes?" he asked as he looked up. Had he really been that absorbed in his menu, or had he simply been giving Momma and me a chance to chat? The man was sweeter than I'd ever given

him credit for when he'd been our chief of police. Either he'd changed over the intervening years or I had.

"How does sweet tea sound to you?" Momma asked him.

"Like a sip of nectar," Phillip said with a smile. "Yes, please."

"Are you ready to order, or do you need more time?" Trish asked us.

"Phillip, are we ready?" Momma asked him.

His gaze returned to the menu. "You two go first. By the time you're finished, I'll be ready."

"Very well," Momma said. "I'll have the lunch soup and sandwich. Roast beef, please."

"Suzanne?" Trish asked.

"I'll take a burger, you know the way I like it, and fries," I said.

"That's what I like, a woman I can depend on," Trish answered. "Chief? How about you?"

"I keep telling you, it's 'Phillip,'" he said. "Now this tuna fish sandwich, is it from a can or is it fresh?"

"The tuna is from a can. Everything else we supply here," she said with a smile.

"Okay, got it. Do you make the chicken Kiev yourself as well?"

"Not me personally, but Hilda does every morning."

"One more question. Are you still serving the Boxcar Special Breakfast Platter, or am I too late for that?"

She glanced at her watch. "The menu changed over to lunch half an hour ago, but for you, we'll make an exception."

"No, that's fine, I was just curious," he said as he finally pushed the menu aside. "I've decided what I want."

"If you'd care to share that news with me, I'll have Hilda whip it up for you," Trish said with a smile.

"After much consideration, I've decided to have a club sandwich, hold the tomato, and an order of French fries."

"An excellent choice," Trish said, still smiling.

"I'm just curious, but would any of the *other* options have been less than ideal?" he asked her, returning her grin with one of his own.

"Not as far as I'm concerned," she said as she left to place our orders with the kitchen.

"What was that about?" Momma asked him after Trish was gone.

"Dot, you're always telling me that it never hurts to explore your options, but there's something to be said for going with the familiar and comfortable choice."

She reached over and patted his hand affectionately. "I think so, too."

"Suddenly I'm wondering if we're still talking about food," he replied with a tender look toward my mother that made me happy she'd been lucky enough to find love twice in her life.

"You just keep on wondering," Momma told him before turning to me. "So, what's our first stop after we leave here? I must admit, I'm excited about the prospect of working with you again."

"Hey, I'll be there too, remember?" Phillip reminded her.

"How could I possibly forget?" she asked him. "Well, Suzanne?"

"I promised Alyssa an update when we spoke last night," I told her. There was no reason to tell Momma and Phillip about the loan Annabeth had made to her mother just before she died. I couldn't imagine the circumstances in which it was pertinent to our investigation. I knew people had killed their loved ones for money before—shoot, I'd even investigated cases like it in the past myself—but if Alyssa had killed Annabeth, I didn't want to be a part of this world anymore.

There were some possibilities that I simply refused to consider.

"Then we'll go there," Phillip said.

"If you don't mind us being present when you speak with her," Momma added.

"Dot, we might not be working this case with Suzanne for very long, but while we're doing it, we're not letting her go somewhere in this investigation without us."

"Even to Alyssa's?" Momma asked.

"Even then," Phillip said. "I'm not saying that I suspect her of killing her own daughter; I just don't think it makes sense to take chances we don't need to take."

"I appreciate that," I said, patting his hand.

"You're more than welcome, but at least half of my reasoning is so I don't have to explain to your husband why I let anything happen to you on my watch," Phillip admitted.

"Still, I appreciate the sentiment," I said as our food arrived.

Momma tried the soup, smiled, and told Trish that it was delicious, and then we all started to eat our meals. There weren't a great many words spoken while we dined. We were all too engrossed in the food in front of us.

Momma deftly snatched the bill from Trish after we finished, and I decided not to fight her for it. I was going to try to be as gracious as George had been when I bought him a donut, though it was still a bit of a struggle for me nonetheless.

We were about to leave when Trish called out, "Suzanne, do you have a second?"

Momma got the hint immediately. "Come, Phillip. Let's take a stroll through the park to work off some of that meal."

"If I do too much exercise, I'm just going to get hungry and have to eat again," he said with a smile. "It's a vicious circle, you know."

"I'm willing to risk it if you are," she said before turning to me. "Suzanne, we'll be outside. Take your time."

"Thanks, Momma," I said. After she and Phillip were gone, I turned to Trish. "What's going on? Is something wrong?"

"Suzanne, you don't think Annabeth's death was an accident, do you?"

CHAPTER 18

"WHY DO YOU SAY THAT?" I asked Trish, trying to put on my best poker face.

"Come on, I've known you too long not to recognize it when you're working on a case, and the only death we've had around here recently is Annabeth's."

"Everyone says that it was an accident," I told her, keeping my voice down so her other diners couldn't hear our conversation. I knew that word would get out soon enough what I was up to, but the longer I could delay it being general knowledge, the better.

"Annabeth didn't fall off that ladder, and we both know it," Trish said. "She was either pushed or she wasn't on it in the first place. How can you tell if someone hits their head falling or if someone knocks them on the back of the noggin instead? I doubt the two acting chiefs could tell them apart, or even Chief Grant, for that matter." She got a little closer as she added, "Suzanne, she was my friend, too. If there's anything I can do to help, I want to do it."

Trish looked as though she were about to cry, a rare show of emotion for her. I knew that she and Annabeth had stayed in touch more than the two of us had. Didn't she have as much right as I did to try to find our friend's killer? "Fine. I don't think it was an accident."

Trish nodded. "Thanks for being honest with me. How can I help?"

"First of all, don't do any prying, I'm doing enough of that myself, but if you overhear anything about Martin Lancaster, Bonnie Small, Kerry Minter, or the artists Galen and Christopho Langer, let me know immediately." I took a deep breath and made sure that I had her full attention. "Trish, it's important that you don't do *anything* to find out about any of them. Let me handle that part of it."

"Why should you get to have all of the fun?" she asked me with a dark smile.

"If you want to help me, and help Annabeth too, you'll do as I ask."

She must have seen how serious I was about my request. "Okay. I get it. The last thing I want to do is make your investigation harder for you. What's the plan, anyway?"

"I'm still trying to figure it out, with a little help from my friends and family. Is it all right with you that I didn't ask you for help earlier?"

"Sure. I just want to be sure that I'm on the list, no matter how far down the chart I might be," she said with a weary smile. "Are you trying to get alibis for the time of the murder from your list of suspects?"

"That's the thing," I said softly. "Nobody seems to know exactly when it happened. There's something like a three-hour window where nobody saw or spoke with Annabeth. When she locked herself in her studio, she cut herself off from the rest of the world." ·

"We know she saw her killer," Trish corrected me. After a moment of thought, she asked, "Is there any other time we can check on that might lead us to the murderer?"

There was only one possible time that might pin down her murderer, though the two events might not have been related, and I realized that I would have to use that to discover any alibis my list of suspects might have. "Last Tuesday night at

ten p.m. behind the library in Union Square, Annabeth was meeting someone. It was in her datebook, and it's the only thing I can come up with that might have something to do with what happened to her. Then again, it might not be related at all. At this point, there's no way to find out."

"Then that's where you need to start. If you can tie the killer in both ways, so much the better, but if it's unrelated, it's going to be good to know that, too. Besides, a three-hour window on the day she was murdered might provide something. If I were you, I'd ask everyone about both."

It was solid reasoning, there was no doubt about that. "Thanks. We're planning to look into both time frames." I touched her shoulder lightly. "I'm sorry you lost such a good friend. I've been so focused on my own loss that I haven't been thinking about anyone else and how they must be feeling right now."

"Hey, you find out who killed her. That's all that matters to anyone who knew and loved Annabeth right now."

I hugged Trish, and to my surprise, she held the embrace longer than I did. When I stepped back, I saw that there were a few customers waiting to pay, but they'd been respecting our moment of grief, and they'd held back.

I nodded. "I'd better go. You've got work to do."

"So do you," Trish said, wiping a tear from the corner of her eye. "Find whoever did this, Suzanne."

"I'll do my best," I said.

Momma and Phillip were outside of the diner, standing in front of Momma's luxury car. "How did that get here?" I asked them.

"We had to get to the donut shop some way," Momma said. "I thought I might drive us during our investigation."

"What's wrong with my Jeep?" I asked.

"Suzanne, everyone in seven counties knows that Jeep. I thought an element of surprise might be nice as a change of pace."

"Besides, this way nobody has to crawl into the back," Phillip said with a smile. "You take shotgun, Suzanne. I *like* having Dot drive me around."

Momma shook her head. "Just for that, I should make *you* drive."

"Hey, it's a win/win for me," he said, trying to suppress his grin. "I'm happy either way."

"Just get in back, Phillip," Momma said.

So it was settled. I wasn't in the mood to fight her about it, and besides, my stepfather was right. It might be nice having my mother drive me around for a change.

After we were all settled in, she started off.

"Where are we going?" I asked her curiously.

"You said you wanted to speak with Alyssa," Momma answered apologetically. "I'm sorry. I should have waited for your instructions."

Momma started to pull over into a parking lot when I said, "No, you're absolutely right. Let's head there first."

When we got there, I noticed that Alyssa's car was gone. "I can't imagine where she must be," I said.

"We can always come back later," Momma said.

"Since we're here, I'd like to see the studio," Phillip said from the back seat.

"I'm sorry, but I don't have the key right now," I answered.

"I can still look in through the windows, can't I? It might help me to visualize the scene."

"Why not?" I asked as I opened my door. "I don't see what it

could possibly hurt." Momma and Phillip followed me, and we walked around the side of the house to the studio.

To my surprise, someone else was already there, though.

"Bonnie, you can't be serious," I said as I confronted Bonnie Small standing in front of the studio's door with a brick in her hands. "Were you really about to break into Annabeth's studio?"

"What? No! Of course not!"

"What's with the brick in your hand, then?" Phillip asked her in his cop voice.

"This? I found it on the ground," she said as she dropped it as though it were suddenly radioactive. The brick fell from her hand and happened to land on her right foot. "Come on," she said in anger. "You've got to be kidding me."

"Bonnie, I'm going to call the police," I told her as I pulled out my phone.

"Why would you do that? I haven't done anything. See for yourself. The door hasn't even been touched!"

"You're still trespassing," Momma said sternly.

"So are you," she countered.

As much as I hated to admit it, she had a point.

"Why are you so intent on getting to those paintings?" I asked.

"I'm representing Annabeth's work," Bonnie said dismissively. "It's my job to see that they are placed with buyers who can appreciate her work."

"Correction: you used to be her agent. We both know that your contract ended the moment she died," I said.

"How could you possibly know that?" Bonnie asked, the fear obvious in her voice.

"Alyssa let Grace read the contract, and there's no way she's ever going to sign a rider to allow you to continue on as her daughter's agent. Face it. It's over."

"Fine," she said, her disgust with the situation now obviously out in the open. "I'm finished, anyway. Not only have I lost Annabeth, but Galen and Christopho have fired me as well. I think I'll go back to Des Moines and try something else. I was happy there once upon a time."

"You're not going to keep being an artistic agent, are you?" I asked her.

"No, I'm finished with temperamental artists and tight-fisted gallery owners. I'm getting out of the business altogether. Maybe I'll become a literary agent instead. I understand that all you have to do is say you are one to start working."

I had heard that there were decent literary agents out there, but I'd never met one, and if Bonnie Small was any indication, they might be few and far between. "Before you leave town, I have a few questions I'd like to ask you."

"No, thanks," she said as she started to brush past me. "I don't have to talk to you anymore. There's nothing I can get out of it."

"Maybe not, but you still have to talk to her," Phillip said as he pulled out his badge that he'd used when he'd been the police chief.

What was he doing? I couldn't let him risk his integrity just to help me out on a case. "Bonnie, he's retired," I said. Phillip gave me a look, but Momma nodded in agreement. If we were going to do this, we were going to do it right.

"That doesn't mean that I can't make a citizen's arrest," Phillip said.

"You don't have any evidence against me about anything," Bonnie answered.

"I have enough to keep you locked up for a few days," he replied. "Who do you think the acting chiefs in town are going to believe, you or me?"

Bonnie seemed to consider the odds of her getting out of

town quickly, and she finally shrugged. "Fine. I don't know anything, but I'll answer your questions truthfully if I can."

I couldn't be certain that the woman wouldn't lie to me, but for the moment, I had to take what I could get. "Where were you last Tuesday night at ten p.m., and then again from noon to three on the day Annabeth died?"

"I am home in bed, alone, on Tuesday and every other day at ten. I can't seem to stay awake past nine these days. As for the day Annabeth died, why do you want to know?" She didn't even wait for an answer. "Is that what this is all about? Do you think someone actually *killed* her? Are you talking about *me?*"

"I'm eliminating suspects right now. Until I learn otherwise, *everyone* involved in Annabeth's life is on my list."

"I suppose I deserve that," Bonnie said. "As it so happens, I can tell you *exactly* where I was. Martin Lancaster and I were going toe to toe about Galen's next exhibit at his gallery. He was demanding a larger percentage of her sales, and I knew that if I took the deal, she'd fire me on the spot. We fought back and forth from a little before eleven until sometime after five when he got a call about Annabeth. As much as I'd love to figure out a way to pin it on him, I'm afraid I'm his alibi."

"And he is yours," Momma said. She then turned to me. "How convenient. Suzanne, is there any way they conspired with each other to protect themselves by supplying mutual alibis?"

"Hey, I'm standing right here," Bonnie protested, clearly annoyed with my mother ignoring her presence.

"You need to hush," Momma said sternly as she turned to the agent for a moment. To my surprise, and Bonnie's as well, she decided to follow the advice and keep quiet.

"No," I said. "Those two hate each other. I can't imagine it."

"We weren't alone at his gallery," Bonnie said testily. "His assistant was there as well, except for the twenty minutes she left the office to get us lunch, and neither one of us could have

driven to April Springs, pushed Annabeth off that ladder, and made it back. Shoot, you can't even drive between Maple Hollow and April Springs one way in that amount of time."

It was true enough, and the alibi was easy enough to check. I doubted Lancaster's assistant would lie to protect him. From my earlier, albeit brief, encounter with her, she'd seemed to have no love for the man at all.

"We're going to check that out, so I hope you're telling the truth," Phillip said sternly.

"I have no reason to lie to you," she said. "Now I'm leaving. You'd better have a set of handcuffs on you if you plan on trying to stop me."

Phillip looked at me, and I shook my head. We'd clearly gotten everything we were going to get out of Bonnie Small, and I didn't want to push it any further.

"That's fine," Phillip said, "but I wouldn't leave town if I were you."

"Then it's a good thing you're not me," Bonnie Small said as she stormed off. I hadn't seen her car when we'd driven up, but evidently she'd parked on the street behind Alyssa's house, and she'd cut through someone's yard to get there unnoticed. If that didn't tell me she was up to no good, then I wasn't sure what would. She wasn't a good agent, or even a decent person, but that didn't make her a killer. Still, I had an alibi to check. I called Marcast gallery, and to my relief, I got the assistant, not the owner. She quickly confirmed the alibi once I reminded her who I was, and when I hung up, Phillip and Momma were staring at me.

"What happened? Did she confirm it?" Phillip asked me.

"She did," I said. "That's two names we can take off our list."

"Unless she's covering for her boss," Phillip said. "I know what you said earlier, but it could all be an act."

"Trust me, you weren't there. The hate she feels for her boss practically radiated off that girl," I answered.

"Why would she continue to work there if she felt that way?" Momma asked, clearly perplexed by the situation.

"Maybe she doesn't feel as though she has any choice," I said.

"Suzanne, there is *always* a choice."

"Maybe between starving and not starving," I said. "I certainly wasn't expecting to have two of my suspects eliminated so quickly today."

"That's what happens when you work with such an outstanding team of investigators," Phillip said with a slight smile.

"Settle down, *Chief*," Momma said. "What was that all about, anyway?"

"I thought we might be able to use my former status as leverage," Phillip admitted reluctantly.

"Are you going to do it again?" my mother asked her husband. He wasn't stupid. "No."

"No what?"

"No, ma'am?" he asked, grinning a bit.

She couldn't keep up her stern expression. "You'll be the death of me someday. You know that, don't you?"

"Maybe, but let's hope that it's not for a very long time," he said as he kissed my mother easily.

The man was good for her, something that I'd hated to admit early on, but it was so obvious now to anyone who knew her before they'd started their courtship and subsequent marriage.

The sweet little scene was interrupted by the sound of someone approaching. I was beginning to think that if we stayed right where we were, sooner or later *everyone* we wanted to talk to would come by.

CHAPTER 19

I T WAS ALYSSA, WHICH SHOULDN'T have surprised me.

"Sorry I wasn't here earlier," she explained. "I wasn't sure what time you were coming by, and I had a few errands I couldn't put off any longer."

"You don't owe me an explanation," I said. "I hope you don't mind, but I asked Momma and Phillip to join us."

"I'm happy to see you all," she said as she addressed them directly. "Let's go inside, shall we?" she asked as she shivered slightly looking at Annabeth's studio. "I can put on a kettle, and we can have some tea."

"That sounds lovely," Momma said smoothly. "I'll help."

I was sure that Alyssa was perfectly capable of making a pot of tea by herself, but she looked pleased to have Momma's company nonetheless.

As Phillip and I waited for them in the living room, he said, "I'm sorry if I pushed the line before."

"And I'm sorry I called you on it," I responded.

"No, you were right to do it. I'm not sure what I was thinking, claiming to be the acting chief of police."

"You never said that, though it was certainly implied by the way you pulled out your old badge, but I know that you were just trying to help," I said as I patted his hand.

Momma and Alyssa soon appeared with a full tea service on

a tray. "How are you two getting on in here?" Momma asked, noting her husband's and my expressions.

"Like gangbusters," Phillip said, smiling at his wife and our hostess.

After we were all served tea, with a few cookies thrown into the mix as well, Alyssa asked, "How is your investigation going? Where is Grace, by the way?"

"She had to leave town suddenly, but we're helping out," Momma said before turning to me. "Suzanne, would you like to bring her up to date?"

I started to recap what we'd been doing, but I hesitated before I told her about eliminating Bonnie Small and Martin Lancaster as primary suspects. It wasn't that I was going to hold the information back. I just wasn't sure how to word it.

"Tell her everything, dear," Momma prompted me gently.

"I'm just trying to figure out how to put it," I said.

"Lancaster and Bonnie Small alibi each other at the time of your daughter's death," Phillip said. I could have been that blunt myself, but I'd been trying to come up with wording that didn't mention Annabeth's murder. It might have seemed to be an odd thing to do, but the woman was hurting, and I didn't want to add anything to her pain if I could help it.

"Forgive my husband's bluntness," Momma said, giving him a mildly reproachful look.

It was clear from his puzzled expression that Phillip had no idea what he'd just done wrong.

"Honestly, he's a breath of fresh air," Alyssa said. "I'm so tired of everyone tiptoeing around me that I could scream. Thank you for your candor, Phillip."

He didn't quite crow at the praise, but it was just as clear that he was pleased by her appreciation of his direct approach.

"What's next?" Alyssa asked me.

"We're going to push our last three suspects as hard as we

dare," I said, being as blunt as my stepfather had been. Maybe the old dog could still teach me a trick or two after all.

"Are you certain one of them killed my baby?" Alyssa asked. She nearly broke down when she said the word *baby*, but somehow she managed to keep it together.

"They are clearly the most obvious candidates," I said. "Don't worry, Alyssa. With any luck, this will all be over soon."

"Forgive me for saying so, but I somehow doubt that," she said sadly.

"My daughter might not be a professional detective, but she certainly has a talent for solving these kinds of cases," Momma said gently.

"I don't doubt Suzanne's abilities," Alyssa said hastily. "I just don't believe that it will ever actually be over. After all, as much as I want to see whoever did this brought to justice, I will take this loss with me to my grave."

The three of us sat in silence for a prolonged pause, and then Alyssa seemed to snap herself out of it. "More tea, anyone?"

"I'd love some," Phillip said as he gulped down whatever was still in his cup.

Alyssa nodded, and as she poured, I nodded my thanks to Phillip. I wasn't saying it was a good thing that Grace had been called away so unexpectedly, but I'd certainly found two good substitutes to take her place until Jake could get home.

After we left Alyssa's place, Momma patted her husband's shoulder. "You're a good man. You know that, don't you?"

"Sure, but I like being reminded that you know, too, every now and then," he said with a grin. "What exactly did I do to merit praise this time?"

"Just being yourself," she said as she returned his smile.

"That I can't help but continue to do," he replied, and then

he turned to me as we walked back to Momma's car. "Suzanne, which of your last three suspects do we tackle next?"

"Honestly, we can discuss it along the way, since all three of them are based in Union Square," I said. "We can probably find Kerry Minter at her art supply house, and with any luck, Galen and Christopho will be at their studios, so it shouldn't be too hard to track them down."

"Then let's go see what we can uncover," Momma said.

After a prolonged discussion, we decided to confront the two artists on our list first. After all, their names had both been in boxes, while Kerry's had been in a bubble. I reminded myself that I could be wrong about the supposition that Annabeth's suspects were in squares only. Kerry had certainly given us enough reason to continue to suspect her, but then again, so had Galen, and upon further examination, so did Chris Langer, or as he liked to be referred to, Christopho, regardless of how they'd been designated.

My cell phone rang as we drove toward Union Square, and I found myself hoping that it was Jake. Instead, I saw Trish's name in the caller ID.

"Hey, Trish. Don't tell me you found something out already."

"I'm not doing anything more than chatting with my customers," she said defensively, so I knew instantly that she'd been doing more than that, but it was a risk I knew I was taking when I'd brought her into the investigation. Trish wasn't the kind of gal who could do *anything* by half measures or sit back and wait in the wings for things to happen, either.

"I hope you're not taking any unnecessary risks on our account," I said.

"Like you do all of the time?" she asked me.

She might be in a playful mood, but I certainly wasn't, not given what was at stake. "What's going on, Trish?" If I wasn't ready to answer her question, then I'd just duck it completely.

"I've got a few friends who know Kerry Minter," she said. "One of them happened to be in the diner...okay, I can't lie to you. I called him. Long ago he told me that he'd dated Kerry five years ago, and I wanted to check her out. I just followed up with him, and he told me something that you need to hear."

"What did he tell you?" I was certainly intrigued.

"He said that Kerry has always been obsessed with the men she was interested in, to the point of being a danger to others."

I'd believed that she was ardent in her pursuit of Chris Langer, but I didn't know how far she might go. "Did he happen to give you any examples?"

"Oh, yes. When he broke up with her because he was interested in someone else—and bear in mind this was after they had gone out on a total of two dates, two dates mind you—Kerry showed up at the other woman's work, hysterical and claiming that she was having his baby, and that the new girl had to butt out before it was too late or she'd end up ruining her baby's life."

It was a chilling thought. "Is it possible that she was telling the truth?"

"If she was having a child, which he sincerely doubted, it certainly wasn't with him. He assured me of that because of an accident in his childhood that made that impossible, and I believe him. Even if that weren't true, he assured me that they hadn't gone much beyond holding hands, though she'd been after him for more. He'd had a suspicion about her, and he'd held back to keep from letting things go any further. He said when the girl he'd been interested in called him in tears to accuse him of getting Kerry pregnant and then abandoning her, she wouldn't believe him when he told her the truth. She told

him that Kerry was too earnest, too believable, and she refused to see him anymore."

"She sounds like a real sociopath," I said, which certainly got Momma and Phillip's attention. I couldn't take time to explain, at least not at the moment. "Thanks, Trish."

"I hope it helps," she said.

"Every piece we add to the puzzle completes the picture a little more," I said.

"Good. I'll keep digging," Trish replied.

"Just keep being careful," I warned her, but I wasn't sure she was even still on the line. I was going to have to be careful of how I used her in the future. I'd had a friend nearly struck down from helping me in the past, and I wasn't about to let it happen again, at least not if there was anything I could do about it.

"Let's go to Artie's instead," I told Momma after I put my cell phone away.

"Is Kerry the psychopath you were just talking about?" Phillip asked from the back seat.

"Actually, I called her a sociopath," I admitted.

After I told them what Trish had shared with me, Momma frowned. "What does that have to do with Annabeth's death?"

"Think about it, Momma. If Kerry went that far to scare off a rival back then, what could she have done to Annabeth? She wanted Chris Langer for herself, and it sounded as though she wouldn't stop until she got him."

"Suzanne, making up a lie and confronting a woman at her workplace is bad, I will grant you that much, but it doesn't make the woman a murderer."

"Unless she's elevated her game," Phillip said. "Dot, you tend to think better of folks than they sometimes deserve. It's

not a horrible trait to have, but when it comes to dealing with the seedier side of life, it can be a real impediment."

"If so, I can live with it," Momma said. "At any rate, let's go speak with the young lady and see what she has to say for herself. She at least deserves that much from us, don't you agree?"

"I think innocent until proven guilty is fine in theory," Phillip said. "I just don't want you to be disappointed if she turns out to have done it."

"If she did, then I'll be pushing to have her punished for what she did more than anyone else. All I'm saying is that we give her a chance."

We didn't get that opportunity, though.

When we got to the art supply shop, no one was there, including the owner.

CLOSED FOR INVENTORY. REOPENING IN SEVEN DAYS.

That was all it said.

"Something's going on," I said. "I've been in this shop recently. Unless she's checking her stock blindfolded, there's no way an inventory could possibly take that long."

Phillip peered inside at the darkened space. "Besides, if she was doing inventory, wouldn't she need to have the lights on? It's as dark as a cave at midnight in there."

"Perhaps you two are missing something," Momma said. "This still doesn't necessarily prove her guilt."

"We never said that it did," I said, rushing to Phillip's and my defense. "Why else do you see her running away, though?"

"First of all, we don't know that she's run anywhere, and

second of all, what if the poor girl is afraid for her life? Whoever killed Annabeth could also be after her."

I had to admit that I hadn't considered that possibility. "Why would anyone want *both* women dead?" I asked.

Momma seemed to ponder that for a bit before answering. "What if Kerry saw or heard something that happened between Annabeth and her killer? Wouldn't *that* put her in jeopardy?"

"If she was a witness to something, she should have come forward the moment she learned about Annabeth's death," Phillip said, spoken like a true former chief of police.

"Maybe she should have, but she could be afraid for her life," Momma said.

"I might be tempted to run if I were in her shoes," I admitted.

"See? Even Suzanne agrees with me," Momma said triumphantly.

"Hold your horses there," I replied. "Just because I see it as a possibility, I also think it's equally likely that she might have been the one to do it."

"All I'm asking is for you both to keep open minds. We need to track her down, so we can determine the reason for her absence ourselves."

"I'll get a friend on it," Phillip said as he took out his cell phone and started to make a call. When he got the party in question, he began a whispered conversation that both Momma and I tried to listen in on, equally unsuccessfully.

"Okay, I've got the word out," Phillip said after he finished his call. "In the meantime, why don't we go to this loft where both of our remaining suspects have studios? If we're in luck, we'll find at least one of them there working."

Momma and I agreed, and after I gave her directions, she quickly found the warehouse space I'd visited earlier.

CHAPTER 20

"IT'S STILL HOT IN HERE," I said as the three of us walked into Chris's, or Christopho's, studio space.

"If the owner doesn't fix it soon, we're going to have a rent strike," he said irritably. "Who have you got with you now?" he asked as he took in Momma and Phillip.

"Allow me to present my mother and her husband," I said.

"Please, call us Dot and Phillip," Momma said as she extended her hand. She paused afterward to take in the work on his easel. It was mostly unchanged since I'd seen it last, although he'd added a few dribbles of red to the canvas in my absence. Was that really all he'd done in all of that time? It must take him forever to produce one painting if that was the normal pace of his work.

"Are you patrons of the arts?" Christopho asked as he cooed to my mother. He clearly was a master at sizing up his visitors. One look at the three of us, and he'd zeroed in on the only one who might be able to appreciate what he was doing, and what was more, be able to afford it.

"I've collected some local artists' work," she admitted. "Mostly Annabeth Kline's in recent history," Momma said. "What do you think of her paintings?"

"Annabeth always had her own distinctive style," Christopho said diplomatically. "She was very good at what she focused on, and we've all lost something by her death."

"Quite different from your work, though," Momma said as she gestured to his current artwork.

"No offense to my late friend and colleague, but if you want a realistic image, take a photograph. I like to deal with deeper issues."

"Such as this?" Momma asked him as she studied the painting a bit more.

"The tumult in man's soul is vastly more interesting to me than what he looks like on the outside," the artist said.

Momma nodded in understanding, but I thought it was a bit of poppycock. It wasn't that I couldn't appreciate abstract art in its many forms, but even Picasso started out rendering things realistically. I've always thought you couldn't break the rules until you mastered them, but what did I know? I was a donut maker, plain and simple, and I never wanted to be anything else for the rest of my life. Maybe Grace and Momma were seeing something on a deeper level that I'd been missing, but if so, I wasn't sure I'd ever learn to appreciate this man's particular style.

"I don't know about that," Phillip said as he stepped up to get a closer look. Momma was about to stop him from speaking, but for some reason, maybe it was something in his expression, she remained silent. "This one makes me uneasy."

"Exactly," Christopho said gleefully. "That's exactly what I've been struggling to attain."

"Well, you can stop, because you're there right now," Phillip said. "To be honest with you, it's not my taste, but I can see the value in it."

"That's all that I ask of anyone," he said, nodding in agreement. "Would you like to know more about my work?" he asked Momma.

"Later, but for the moment, we're collecting the thoughts and movements of Annabeth's friends and colleagues before she died. We know you two were friends, so I'm sure you won't

mind helping us put something together. It's for her mother, you understand. I'm sure if the roles were reversed, you'd like someone to do it for yours."

It was a brilliant stroke adding Alyssa into the mix, one only a mother would think of, I thought.

"I'll do what I can," he said.

Momma gestured to me, so I asked him our planned questions. "The first date, the Tuesday before her death, at ten p.m. is what we're asking everyone to remember and share."

Christopho frowned at me for a moment before he responded. "That's an oddly specific time," he said.

"Evidently it's horoscope-star-chart stuff," Phillip blurted out.

"Pardon me?" Christopho asked. Had my stepfather lost his mind?

If he had, he was continuing with the charade, doubling down. "One of Annabeth's friends is big into astrology, and she said that if she knew where folks were and what they were doing twice during the last week of Annabeth's life, she could tell Alyssa things that no one has any right to know. I don't put much stock in it myself, but you never know."

"No, you don't," the artist said. "Okay. Let's see. The Tuesday before at ten p.m., I was here working."

"Did anyone see you?" I asked.

"No, not that I'm aware of, but when I'm in the zone of creation, you could set a bomb off under me and I wouldn't even hear it."

So, we were zero for one. "How about at the moment she died? We can't pin it down much between noon and three p.m. that day. Any luck there?"

I was hoping for something, but I was destined to be disappointed yet again. "Can't say that I know that one, either. I'm sorry. I won't be able to help your project after all." He then

turned back to Momma and said, "If you're interested, I've got some things from my rose period you might like."

"You painted roses?" I asked him, wondering if you could even tell they were flowers, based on the work I was looking at.

"Not the flower, the tone and the hue," he said dismissively.

"Let's make an appointment next week to get together," Momma told him.

Christopho seemed overly pleased by the offer. "That would be grand."

"Very well. I'll call you later to iron out the details. In the meantime, would you know if Galen is in her studio?"

"You're interested in *her* work?" he asked incredulously. "It's a bit derivative if you ask me."

"We're working on that astral chart, remember?" I asked.

"Oh, yes. Of course. She has a separate entrance. You go back outside and use the stairwell to the top floor. If she's there, her door will be open, despite the chill in the air today."

"Thank you," I said.

As soon as we were outside again, I turned to Phillip and Momma. "I knew you were an art lover," I said to my mother, "but you surprised me," I added as I looked at my stepfather.

"My tastes may be simple, but I know what I like," Phillip said, "and that work in there wasn't it. It gave me the willies just looking at it. I'd no sooner own it than I would a portrait of a serial killer. No, that's not true. I'll take the serial killer hands down, every last time."

"I'm not sure I'd take either one, but I get your point," I said. As we climbed the stairs after ascertaining that Galen's door was open, I asked Momma, "Were you serious about viewing his other work?"

"Suzanne, a closed mind opens no doors."

"What's that supposed to mean?" I asked. "Are you suddenly spouting off in fortune cookies?"

Momma just shook her head, a reaction I'd been known to get from her quite often over my lifetime and something I'd grown used to.

If Christopho's studio had been hot, Galen's was absolutely scorching. Despite the weather outside, she was dressed in the merest of short, tight skirts and a top that was barely decent. The woman had a great body, I had to give her that much, even if I didn't personally care for her multiple piercings. Phillip did his best not to notice, a fact that I was certain Momma would appreciate. I supposed if I looked like that, I might be tempted to dress that way as well, but neither event was ever going to happen. I caught him sneaking a few quick glances in her direction, but I decided he was allowed, at least as far as I was concerned. Momma might be another matter altogether.

Galen smiled at us until she recognized me. "What are you doing here?"

"Looking for information," I said. "This is my mother and her husband. They are art fans."

"Okay," she said, dialing her hostility back a bit. To be fair, if I had to work in that kind of heat for more than a few minutes, I'd probably be angry all of the time, too.

There wasn't a current work in progress on display and her hands were free of paint, which I thought was odd, particularly given the studios of the other artists we'd seen. "Where's your artwork?" I asked her.

"I'm getting ready for a show I don't want to have," she said with a frown, "not that it's any of your business. Now why are you here?"

"We're trying to put together an astrological footprint for Annabeth's death for her mother," Momma told her. I myself didn't think there was anything to astrology in general, but then

again, once upon a time I'd taken part in cleansing the bookstore space before Paige Hill had opened for business, and I'd felt a palpable difference before and after the burning sage ritual, so what did I know? Like Momma had just reminded me, normally having an open mind is not necessarily a bad thing.

"I don't believe in that rubbish, lady," she said curtly to my mother.

Phillip may have been temporarily smitten by Galen's physical appearance, but the moment she'd disrespected my mother, he'd lost even a cursory interest in her. "Fine. We'll do it the hard way. Where were you last Tuesday night at ten p.m. and then again on the day of Annabeth's death between noon and three p.m.?"

"You sound just like a cop," she said, and not like it was a good thing.

"That's because I am, or I should say, I used to be. Chief of police. Answer the questions, or do you have something to hide?"

"My life is an open book," she said, though I doubted it was true. "If you're retired, why should I talk to you at all?"

"I might not be on the force anymore," Phillip said coolly, "but I'm sure I could make your life interesting if I put my mind to it. It's fine with me either way. Your call."

She studied him a moment, and then she threw her hands into the air. "It's too hot to play cat and mouse with you, especially when I have nothing to hide. As a matter of fact, I was with a patron of the arts on both occasions."

"He can confirm this?" Phillip asked.

"It's a she, and yes, she can if she has to," Galen said. "I won't give you her name without a court order, though."

"That's your decision," Phillip said.

"It's fine. I'll call Benjamin myself," Momma said as she reached for her phone.

"Wait," Galen said, suddenly squirming in discomfort, though it had nothing to do with the heat. "How did you know about us?"

"I thought you said you were seeing a woman," I said.

"If you'll think about it, that's not what I said at all," Galen answered. "I just didn't see any satisfaction in telling you the truth." She turned back to Momma. "I want to know how you found out."

"My dear, your secret is safe with us. Benjamin and I are on a few boards together. We've known each other for years, and a few weeks ago, we were at a cocktail party and he'd had a little too much to drink. He described you quite eloquently, said he hadn't felt so young and alive in years thanks to you, and then he realized that he'd said too much. One phone call is all it will take to confirm that you're telling the truth."

To my surprise, Galen crumpled and began to cry. "If you call him, he'll end it with me. He warned me that if it ever happened, it would be the last I ever saw of him, and that he'd deny we'd ever met."

Even more of a shock, Momma moved to her and put her arms around the artist. Galen seemed to resist it at first, but the person who could willingly keep out of my mother's embrace hadn't been born yet, at least as far as I was concerned. "He's a cad, my dear, and I'm certain you can do better."

"I thought you said that you were friends," Galen told her, wiping away a few tears.

"I said we'd known each other for years, but friendship? Not hardly. Is there anything I can do to help?"

"No, ma'am, I'll be okay," she said as she pulled away. "Maybe you're right. It could be that it's time I stood on my own two feet."

"I know it is," Momma said reassuringly. She pulled out a card and held it out to Galen. "If you need to talk, call me."

I hadn't seen her do that more than half a dozen times in my entire life. After I recovered, I said, "We won't bother you anymore."

"Do you promise that you won't call him?" Galen asked, almost pathetically. The hard and icy exterior had suddenly been replaced by the insecure young girl that seemed to live just beneath the surface.

"We promise," Momma said. "And no matter what it takes, get this heat situation fixed."

"I've tried, but Benjamin thinks it's funny," Galen said.

"As I said, he's unworthy of you," Momma replied.

Once we were outside again climbing down the stairs, I felt the relief from the cold as the sweat crystalized on my face. "How did you know about her and that man?" I asked her.

"Please, Suzanne. The young woman is distinctive if nothing else, especially around here. From the moment I saw her, I knew that she was Benjamin's secret paramour."

"So, we aren't going to call to confirm her alibi?" Phillip asked grudgingly. "That breakdown may have been a little too convenient, if you know what I mean."

Momma waited until we were back on the ground before she turned to her husband. "If our other leads don't pan out, we may have to call him yet, but honestly, I believe her, and I don't want to be the reason that relationship implodes, if that's what you can call what they are having." She paused a moment and then smiled. "I must say, your restraint was admirable, dear."

"I don't know what you're talking about," Phillip said hastily.

"I'm sure you don't," Momma said with a twinkle in her eye.

At that moment, my cell phone rang. Was Trish calling me with another update? She was busier than I was on the case.

Better yet, it was Jake!

CHAPTER 21

"How's your drive so far?" I asked him.

"Honestly, I'm making better time than I expected," he admitted.

"I wasn't sure your old truck could even *go* over the speed limit," I answered with a laugh. I knew that I was in the middle of a serious investigation, but I was downright giddy about the prospect of Jake making it back home to me.

"I know I told you I'd be home this evening, but I'm almost to Union Square. Is that enough notice for you, or should I kill a little time before I drive the rest of the way home?"

"I'm in Union Square with Momma and Phillip!" I squealed.

"Where, exactly?"

"Tell you what. Meet us in Napoli's parking lot. I can't wait to see you."

"Suzanne, I haven't been gone that long," Jake answered.

"I know, but it feels like forever to me."

"Me, too," he said. "See you soon."

After I hung up, Momma started driving. "We're meeting Jake at Napoli's, right?"

"Yes, he really made good time."

"I'll wager he's been ignoring the speed limit," Momma said.

"Can you blame him, if he's coming to see me?" I asked her with a grin.

"No cop's going to pull him over," Phillip said.

"Because he used to be a state police investigator?" I asked him.

"No, it's because they'd be too embarrassed to flag that old truck of his for speeding," my stepfather answered with a grin.

Evidently we were closer to Napoli's than Jake was, because he wasn't in the parking lot yet. I looked at Momma and Phillip and said, "I can't tell you how much I appreciate you both working on this with me."

"But we're fired now, right?" Phillip asked with a grin.

"Let's just say that your temporary duty has been completed. It sounds so much nicer that way," I answered, hoping that I wasn't hurting their feelings. They were good helpers, but when it came to dealing with murder, either Jake or Grace would be my first choice, and if I was being one hundred percent honest about it, Jake would edge out my best friend, though just by a hair. I'd had more experience working with Grace on murder investigations, but there was something really complementary about the way my husband and I worked together, though I'd never admit it to anyone else.

"We're not offended, dear," Momma said with a smile. "The truth is that it felt good to be included, if only for a bit. Do you have any idea what you two are going to do next?"

"I think we have to track Kerry Minter down," I said. "Something tells me she might hold the key to this whole thing. If she's hiding from someone, she might be hard to find, but between Jake and me, I feel as though we at least have a shot at it."

"I'm sure you do," Momma said. "If you need us, remember, we're never more than a phone call away."

"I know, and I greatly appreciate it," I said as I spotted Jake's beat-up old pickup truck. "Thanks again," I said as I jumped out.

I barely waited for his truck to stop rolling before I jumped

into the passenger seat and gave him the best hug I could manage. I looked up to see Momma and Phillip waving, and as they drove off, presumably back to April Springs, I realized yet again how lucky I was to have both of them in my lives. If I had anything in this world, I had people who loved me, and that meant more to me than any untold riches ever could.

"Where to?" he asked as he looked at me expectantly. "I assume we're going to keep working on Annabeth's murder together, though you never formally asked me."

"Jake Bishop, would you do me the honor of serving as my co-investigator into Annabeth Kline's murder?" I asked with every bit of pomp and circumstance I could muster.

"Sure, why not?" he asked with a grin. "I'm all yours. Bring me up to speed."

"We've got it narrowed down to two main suspects," I explained. "One of them has no alibi for either the rendezvous with Annabeth behind the library or the time of her murder."

"Which one might that be?"

"Chris Langer, though he likes to be referred to as *Christopho*," I said.

"Sounds nice and pretentious. What about the other one?"

"It's Kerry Minter."

"What does she have to say for herself?" Jake asked me.

"I don't know. We couldn't find her to ask," I admitted.

After explaining about the note we'd found on her shop's door claiming that she had inventory though no one was there, I said, "My thought is we need to find her, no matter what it takes."

"I'm good with that," Jake said. "Let me make a few phone calls."

"Jake, I don't have to remind you that you aren't working in any official capacity on this, do I? Phillip has already made a few calls himself."

"Suzanne, when I was the April Springs chief of police, I banked enough favors around the area to use for years to come," he said.

"Why would they reciprocate if you're not in office anymore?" I asked him.

"It's a matter of pride with them—and with me, too. Don't worry. I'll get to the bottom of this in record time."

Before he could make the first phone call, I put a hand on his arm. "Jake, I'm sorry about the way things ended up with Tommy."

"No worries, Suzanne. I did everything I could, but since nobody wanted my help or my advice, leaving was the best thing I could do."

"Well, I for one welcome your assistance," I told him solemnly.

"I'm glad," he said. "If you don't mind, I'm going to step out of the truck while I make these calls."

"I don't mind a bit," I replied. I was used to Jake needing privacy on the phone, especially when he was calling in old favors. It gave me time to wonder what on earth Kerry Minter was thinking, bolting like she did. While it was barely possible that her inventory explanation had been the truth, I sincerely doubted it. Either she was running away because she was afraid, or she was guilty of murder, and at that point, I had no idea which one it might be.

Jake got back into the truck and started driving. "She's at her best friend's house—at least she was as of twenty minutes ago."

"How on earth did you discover that so quickly?" I asked as I fastened my seat belt.

"Kerry's housesitting for a friend of the police chief here, and he's the one who just got her settled in. If we hurry, we should be able to catch her there."

The only problem was that she wasn't there when we got to the address in question.

"This doesn't make any sense," Jake said. "I thought for sure she'd be here."

"Let's try someplace else," I said. I gave him Kerry's address, and we drove there without much hope of finding her.

To my surprise, there was a car out front of the house.

A red car, to be exact.

"Be careful, Jake. She might be dangerous," I whispered.

"I'm always careful," he said as we approached the door. I noticed that he pulled out his weapon, which was fine by me. Better to be safe than sorry.

As I started to knock, Kerry nearly ran me down. She was clutching two suitcases, one in each hand, and she looked as though she'd seen a ghost.

"Going somewhere?" I asked her. "I couldn't help noticing your red car in the driveway. That was the same color of the one that nearly ran Annabeth down in front of Martin Lancaster's gallery just before she died."

"I hadn't heard about that," she said, clearly distracted. "Anyway, that's not mine. I just borrowed it from my sister. I didn't want anyone to know what I was driving."

"What are you running from?" I asked her as Jake moved to block her exit. I noticed that he'd put his weapon into his jacket pocket, but I was sure that it was still accessible.

"He's after me," Kerry said, looking wildly around to see if she could spot her hunter.

"Who are you talking about?" Jake asked her.

"Chris Langer. I can't believe I had a crush on him once. The man is a sociopath."

"Why do you say that?" I asked her.

She asked, "Can I put these in the car first?"

Jake reached out both hands. "I'll take care of those for you." She couldn't get away, but why take any chances? "What happened?"

"I asked him out again this afternoon, and he went ballistic. He started screaming at me. 'Why can I get what I don't want, but I couldn't have what I really wanted? She turned me down one too many times, and she paid for it.' It was positively scary. Then he backed me up against the wall and pinned my wrists together. 'This is the last time I'm telling you this. I don't want you. Not now, not ever, so get it through your head before I have to teach you a lesson I guarantee you aren't going to like.' The way he looked into my eyes, I knew he wasn't joking. He was going to kill me if I pushed him again, just like he did Annabeth."

"Did he actually say that?" I asked her.

"Not in so many words, but the meaning was clear enough. Listen, I've gone overboard in the past about men in my life, but my therapist has helped me resolve all of those issues. I know when it's time to cut my losses."

"That's it, then? You're just running away?" I asked her.

"My store isn't worth it, and neither is my time in Union Square. I'm getting as far away from here as fast as I can."

"You need to tell the police here what happened first," Jake said. "They need to know."

"I'm stopping off at the station on my way out of town," she admitted. "Do you think I want this guy to come after me? He told me that if he ever saw me again, he'd kill me!"

"Why don't I come with you to the station?" Jake offered.

"Thanks, but I need to do this alone," she said.

"Aren't you going to lock your front door?" I asked as she started to hurry toward her car.

"If anyone wants anything I left behind, they're welcome to it," she said. "Good-bye."

"Be safe," I said as we watched her drive away.

"Should we follow her to be sure she goes to the station?" Jake asked me.

"Maybe, but what I really want to do is go talk to Chris Langer," I admitted. "It's not that far, and I could go on foot if you want to tail Kerry."

"She can take her chances," Jake said. "You're the only one I have any interest in protecting."

"Then let's go," I said.

Despite the heat I knew was radiating inside the studio, Langer's door was closed, though I could see lights on inside.

"Something's wrong," I told Jake as I headed for the entrance.

"How do you know?" he asked me.

"That studio is boiling hot. If he's in there, he must be roasting."

Jake put a hand on my arm and pulled out his weapon. "Let me go first."

"Okay, but I'm right on your heels. Be careful."

"I will," he said as he pulled out his handgun again.

As he pushed the door open, the place looked as though a struggle had gone on inside. Where it had once been neat and tidy, now it was a real mess, with easels and paintings strewn across the space and tubes of paint thrown everywhere, leaving a real mess.

I was still taking the scene in when Jake said, "Suzanne. Over here."

I looked up to see Jake kneeling over a man's body, clearly checking for a pulse.

Evidently someone had decided that Christopho Langer had painted his last piece of artwork, too.

It was starting to look like open season on artists in our area.

"Is he dead?" I asked as I knelt beside him.

"No, his pulse is still strong, but I'm guessing that somebody clobbered him with that chunk of rock," Jake said as he pointed to the doorstop I'd seen on my earlier visit to his studio. It horrified me when I saw that some of the pieces of protruding quartz were now coated with blood.

"Call an ambulance," Jake said, but as I reached for my cell phone, another voice from behind us countered that order.

"Put that down, Suzanne. Jake, drop that gun or I'm going to have to kill you both."

Evidently Kerry Minter hadn't been running away from anything after all.

CHAPTER 22

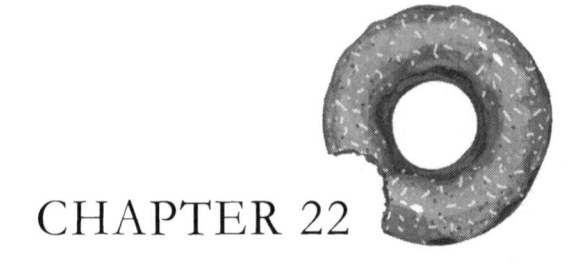

"YOU FOLLOWED US HERE," I said as I hit the panic button on my phone before I dropped it. It was set to call 9-1-1. I just hoped they got it in time to stop this woman from killing us both.

"Push it over here," she ordered.

I didn't have much choice. I slid the phone toward her, hoping that she didn't pick it up to see who I'd just called. Instead of leaning down, though, she lashed out with her heel and smashed it.

Had the call gone through, or had she killed it just as completely as she'd evidently killed Annabeth Kline?

"Jake, I'm not going to tell you again. If you still have that gun in your hand by the time I count to three, I'm going to shoot your wife."

He hesitated, and I whispered, "Don't do it, Jake. She's going to kill us anyway."

He stared at me for a brief second, and then he shrugged as he dropped his weapon to the floor. Jake might have just sealed our fates, but at least this way, we might have a fighting chance if my call had gone through. I had all the faith in the world in my husband's ability to win a shoot-out with the art supply shop owner, but she had the drop on us, and by the time Jake could have pivoted and gotten off a shot, one of us would probably be dead.

"Did you honestly kill her just so you could have Chris to yourself?" I asked her.

"That was part of the reason," Kerry admitted. "I am so much prettier than she ever was. Why would he want *her* instead of *me*?"

"Maybe he was looking for more than just looks," Jake said.

I saw Kerry's finger tighten on the trigger, and I knew that provoking her was not the right way to handle this, not if we wanted a chance of getting out of it alive. "Kerry, it's impossible to know why some people are attracted to others. What I don't understand is why you asked Annabeth to meet you at the library after hours. Why take the chance of being seen together in public if you were just going to kill her?"

"It's probably because she hadn't decided to kill her yet," Jake said. "You were going to give her one last chance to back off, weren't you?"

"It was the right thing to do," I heard the killer say, as if she had any idea what the right thing was any more. "She had talent, money, and Chris. What made matters worse was that she didn't even want him," Kerry said, gesturing to the man's body. The artist hadn't made a single movement since we'd arrived, and I had to wonder if his injuries were more significant than we knew. He had to get help soon, or he might be dead as well. "When I asked her to give him up, she said he wasn't hers to give. She told me I was better than that, that I should actually find someone who wanted me, not someone who didn't care if I was dead or alive. When she walked off, I decided right then and there to kill her."

"But you weren't ready, were you?" Jake asked her.

"I was ready. I just wasn't prepared. I stole this gun from my cousin, and I went to her studio to make sure she didn't bat those eyelashes at Chris ever again."

"But you didn't shoot her," I said, trying to draw her out as much as I could. Right now keeping her talking was our best option.

"I was going to, but she'd left her door unlocked, and she was so wrapped up in a painting she was doing that she didn't even see me come in. I grabbed a paperweight and hit her on the side of the head as hard as I could. It had a ninety-degree angle to it, and I was about to leave it when I noticed that it matched the edge of her worktable. I dragged her to where I thought she might fall if she slipped from the ladder she was on, and then I smeared a little blood and hair from where I hit her onto the table's edge." She shivered slightly. "It was pretty gruesome doing that, but I had no choice."

"That wasn't the first time you wanted to kill her though, was it?" I asked. "I'm willing to bet that if Jake were to check that car's registration, he'll discover that it belongs to you, not your sister."

"I wasn't trying to kill her then. I just wanted to scare her. That's why I pushed those boxes over, too."

"Did you loosen the rung of the ladder, too?" I asked.

She looked surprised by the question. "No, if it's loose, I didn't do it. It looked pretty old to me when I pulled it down."

Most of Annabeth's clues had been spot on, so it hardly mattered if she'd found the loose ladder rung and had decided that someone was trying to kill her that way.

"What about the art she gave me? You broke into the donut shop, and then you tried getting into our cottage. Why?"

"After I killed her, I saw the notes she made on that butcher paper. I had to wonder what else she might have written, and she'd told me about giving you something that would shake your world up. I didn't know what that meant, but I had to find out for myself. What was it?"

"I'd show you a photo of it, but you just broke my phone," I said. Why hadn't the police responded to my call yet? Were we going to die here in Chris Langer's studio alongside him?

"Enough talk," she said. "I'm sorry, but if you two hadn't

been so nosy, you wouldn't be in this predicament in the first place, so in a very real way, it's nobody's fault but your own."

"Do you honestly believe that the police aren't going to track you down after they discover our bodies?" I asked. The question gave me chills as I asked it. If and when that happened, it would be too late for us, and that was what mattered at the moment.

"They won't suspect a thing. After all, it's going to be murder-suicide," she said with a laugh as though she'd just said something amusing. The woman had really snapped.

"I don't see it," Jake said with a frown.

"You confronted Christopho, he shot you both, and then he killed himself," she said.

"How are you going to explain his caved-in skull?" Jake asked.

"I don't have to. Let the police figure it out," she answered. "I'll be long gone by then."

I wasn't sure how long Chris Langer had been awake and listening to us, but he clearly understood that he had to act now or lose the opportunity forever. He reached out for the same baseball-sized rock Kerry had used to bash his head in, and he somehow managed to heave it at her while still lying on his side, suffering from, at the very least, a concussion, and who knew what other damage she'd done on her earlier assault?

She was caught off guard by the rock being heaved at her, and that was all of the distraction we needed. Jake grabbed his weapon, and before Kerry could lift her own, he had her dead to rights.

"Drop it, Kerry. It's over."

I saw her hesitate just as the door opened again behind her. There stood a uniformed cop, his weapon drawn as well. "Drop your weapon," he screamed at her.

It was enough to push her over the edge. I saw her tense as

she got ready to fight and die, and then, as suddenly as it had come, she dropped her gun to the floor and started sobbing.

Apparently the killer decided that it was better to be a live coward than a dead martyr to a cause that no one else in the world cared about.

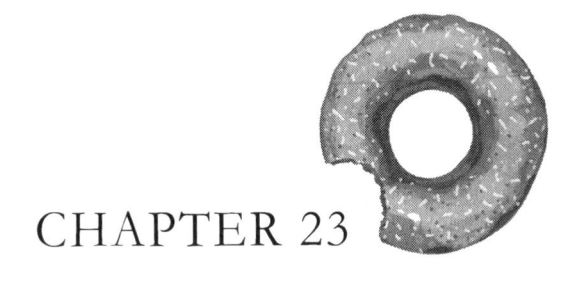

CHAPTER 23

A WEEK LATER, JAKE AND I were settling in for the night at the cottage when the doorbell rang. My husband offered to get the door, but I was closer, so I opened it myself to find three dozen people standing outside on our front porch, all of them grinning like crazy people.

"What's going on?" I asked them in surprise.

Momma was at the front of the crowd. "We know you didn't want us to make any fuss about you coming back home, but now that you've been here for awhile, we decided it would be a good time to have a Happy Thursday party for you."

I had to laugh as I turned to my husband. "Jake, did you know about this?"

"Me?" he asked as innocently as he could manage. "How could you even think such a thing?" It was pretty clear that he'd been in on it all along. I should have known something was up when I'd told him I was going to change into my pajamas for the night and he'd insisted that I stay dressed.

"Well, what are you all out there standing around in the cold for? Come on in," I said as I stepped aside.

Trish, Emma, and Hilda started carrying in food, George, Grace, Max, and Emily all had various decorations they couldn't wait to put up, and Phillip waved an old CD player. "I've got music," he said gleefully.

Before I had time to catch my breath, the party was in full

swing, and I found myself happy that they'd done this behind my back and against my express wishes.

Soon the furniture had all been moved to the edges of the room, and there was actually space enough for an impromptu dance floor.

When one of my favorite songs started playing, Jake offered me his hand. "May I have this dance?"

"You bet," I said as I melted into his arms.

"You're not upset with us, are you?" he whispered softly in my ear. "So many people love you that they couldn't bear the thought of not showing you directly."

"It's wonderful," I admitted. "I love them, too." I stopped dancing for a moment and pulled back. I looked intently into my husband's gaze. "Jake, I never want to leave April Springs."

"I get it, and I agree. It's where we belong," he said.

With that, I pulled him close to me again and continued to dance with the man of my dreams.

I knew, now more than ever, that life, even when it was full of hardships and tragedies, was best lived among those I cared about. Somehow the lows weren't as low, and the highs were even higher when I was around people I loved, and for that brief and shining moment in time, I had so much joy inside me that my heart nearly burst from it all.

I was home in every way that it counted, and that was really all that mattered to me.

RECIPES

A Nice Raised Donut

This recipe is as good a place to start as any if you've never made donuts before. You can adjust the amount of cinnamon and nutmeg if you'd like, but these amounts are my favorites from experimenting over the years. This recipe only goes through one raising period, so it's one of the easier full donut recipes to knock out when you just don't have time for two.

Ingredients

- 1 cup water, warm
- 2 packages fast-rising yeast (1/2 ounce total)
- 2 1/2 tablespoons white granulated sugar
- 1 egg, beaten
- 1/3 cup butter or margarine, melted
- 1 teaspoon cinnamon
- 1 teaspoon nutmeg
- 1 teaspoon vanilla extract
- 1/2 teaspoon salt
- 3–4 cups flour

Directions

In a large mixing bowl, add the water, yeast, and sugar. Give the yeast 5 minutes to start working, and if it doesn't foam up or at

least bubble a little, try fresher yeast. Add the beaten egg, melted butter, cinnamon, nutmeg, vanilla, and salt and then blend it all together thoroughly by hand. Next, start adding flour to the mix, stirring along the way, until the dough pulls away from the sides and is not sticky to the touch. Turn the dough out onto a lightly floured surface and knead the dough for about 2 minutes. Roll it out until it is around ¼ inch thick and cut out any shapes you'd like. We use rounds, diamonds, and even our ravioli cutter, which leaves cool edges.

Cover and let rise in a warm place for approximately one-half hour. While you are waiting, heat enough canola oil to 360 degrees F. Once they've completed their rise time, fry the donuts for approximately 2 to 3 minutes on each side or until golden brown.

Drain on a rack with paper towels underneath and then dust with confectioners' sugar or make up your own simple glaze.

No quantities given, since these depend entirely on the shapes you choose!

The "When All Else Fails" Donut

Okay, let's start with a full disclosure on this one. A friend shared this recipe with me years ago and urged me to make it and see for myself how great they were. I could barely choke the things down, but she tasted them and continued to rave about them. I've made them again a few times over the years, mostly when I know she'll be around, but make these at your own risk. Who knows, you might just have better luck than I have, which isn't really saying much at all! You've been warned! At least it's easy to make, and pretty inexpensive, too.

Ingredients

- 1/2 cup boxed biscuit flour
- 1/2 cup milk (or water if you don't have milk on hand)
- 1 tablespoon white granulated sugar
- 1 teaspoon cinnamon

Directions

Start by heating enough canola oil on the stovetop to fry your donuts. I like to do most of my frying at 360 degrees F.

The recipe itself couldn't be easier. In a large bowl, mix the boxed biscuit flour, milk, sugar, and cinnamon until thoroughly incorporated.

Once your oil is up to temperature, drop teaspoons of batter into the pot, being careful not to splash any oil as you do. These usually take about 2 minutes for the first side and then another minute or two for the other side. You need to keep a close eye on these once they are being fried, because they can go from done to burned in a blink of an eye.

By my count, these make about 18 donuts, a little on the small size. You can dip these in chocolate, drown them in confectioners' sugar, or eat them plain.

One Two Three Donuts!

I call these One Two Three Donuts because they are so easy to make, and unlike the recipe above, the results are outstanding. With just two ingredients, it's ready made for the noncook or nonbaker. In fact, I often tell folks that it's the *perfect* donut recipe for someone who doesn't think they could ever make donuts.

Give it a try, and don't be afraid to vary the liquid you add when you make them again. In the past, in lieu of plain milk, I've used half-and-half, heavy cream, as well as chocolate milk and even eggnog!

No matter what you do, remember to have fun! After all, that's what donut making really should be about.

Ingredients

- 1 packet Martha White chocolate chip muffin mix (7.4 oz.), split in half
- 1/2 cup whole milk (2% can be substituted, or the choices listed above as well)

Directions

These honestly couldn't be simpler.

First, preheat your oven to 350 degrees F. Next, combine the mix with the liquid of your choice, though I'd probably advise making them the first time with whole or 2% milk.

Once mixed together thoroughly, you can add the batter to a donut pan or even use a cupcake pan if that's all you have on hand.

These need to bake approximately 10 to 13 minutes, depending

on your oven. I rely more on inserting a clean toothpick into the center of a few than actual time.

When the toothpick comes out clean, cool them on a rack, and then ice them, dust them with confectioners' sugar, or eat them plain with a glass of milk or a cup of coffee.

Makes 4 to 8 donuts, depending on your pans.

Donuts with a Kick

This is an old favorite of my family, but I won't lie to you. I stole it from our local county fair! The man there was extremely secretive about his recipe, but it didn't take much effort on my part to crack the code when I got back home. These donuts are not only bright and bold in color, they taste that way, too. This recipe is a real hit with kids of all ages, so give them a try when you're feeling adventurous!

Ingredients

Mixed
- 1 egg, lightly beaten
- 3/4 cup white granulated sugar
- 2 tablespoons butter, melted
- 1 teaspoon vanilla extract

Sifted
- 2 cups flour, unbleached all-purpose
- 1 full packet of powdered unsweetened Kool-Aid mix (.13 oz.) Any flavor works for these, but we like Tropical Punch!
- 1 tablespoon baking powder
- Dash of salt
- Canola oil for frying (the amount depends on your pot or fryer)

Directions

Heat enough canola oil on the stovetop to fry your donuts, bringing it up to 360 degrees F.

Next, in a large bowl, beat the egg and then add sugar, butter, and vanilla. Mix this all together and then set it aside. In another bowl, sift together the flour, Kool Aid packet, baking powder,

and salt. Once that is completed, add the dry ingredients to the wet, stirring as you go, until you have a smooth consistency. Be warned, the dye in the Kool-Aid will most likely make these things brighter than anything you've ever baked in your life! Be brave and forge ahead, though.

Next, when the oil has reached the proper temperature, drop walnut-sized balls of dough into the oil. Fry for two to four minutes, turning them halfway through the process.

In my opinion, these don't need any embellishments, but if you'd like, feel free to up the sugar content and dust them with confectioners' sugar.

Makes 10 to 12 donuts, depending on your portions.

A Good Donut for the End of the Day

This donut is a good place to end your day. When it's time to wrap everything up and you can't find anything sweet in the house that appeals to you, give these a try. They are simple to make, give you good results, and when all is said and done, you'll be happy you made them.

Ingredients

- 4–5 cups unbleached all-purpose flour
- 1 cup white granulated sugar
- 1 teaspoon baking soda
- 1/2 teaspoon nutmeg
- 1/2 teaspoon cinnamon
- 2 dashes of salt
- 1 egg, beaten
- 1/2 cup sour cream
- 1 cup buttermilk

Directions

Heat enough canola oil on your stovetop to cover your donuts plus a little more. Bring the oil up to 360 degrees F and then get started on your dough.

In a large bowl, sift the flour, sugar, baking soda, nutmeg, cinnamon, and salt until incorporated. Add the beaten egg, sour cream, and buttermilk, stirring it all lightly in until combined.

Turn the dough out onto a lightly floured surface and knead lightly for approximately 1 minute. Roll the dough out to ¼-inch thickness, then use a donut cutter with the removable donut hole insert to cut out your donuts and holes. If you don't have

this tool, you can use one medium-sized glass for the perimeter, and one a fourth of its diameter to cut out the hole.

Fry the donuts and holes for 2 minutes on each side, flipping halfway through. Take them out of the oil and drain on a rack and serve. For these donuts, I like to take softened butter and spread lightly across the tops, then sprinkle a sugar/cinnamon mix (one tablespoon sugar to one teaspoon cinnamon) while they are still warm.

This recipe makes approximately 1 dozen donuts and matching holes.

If you enjoy Jessica Beck Mysteries and you would like to be notified when the next book is being released, please visit our website at jessicabeckmysteries.net for valuable information about Jessica's books, and sign up for her new-releases-only mail blast.

Your email address will not be shared, sold, bartered, traded, broadcast, or disclosed in any way. There will be no spam from us, just a friendly reminder when the latest book is being released, and of course, you can drop out at any time.

If you enjoy Jessica Beck Mysteries and you would like to be notified when the next book is being released, please visit our website at jessicabeckmysteries.net for valuable information about Jessica's books, and sign up for her new-releases-only mail blast.

Your email address will not be shared, sold, bartered, traded, broadcast, or disclosed in any way. There will be no spam from us, just a friendly reminder when the latest book is being released, and of course, you can drop out at any time.

OTHER BOOKS BY JESSICA BECK

.

Made in the USA
San Bernardino, CA
22 January 2020